Dedication

To the men and women who served in the shadows that we could sleep in safety.

Acknowledgements

The names of places and events used in this story are based on historical fact. The names of characters are, however, are entirely fictitious and products of the Author's imagination. Any resemblance to any person living or deceased is purely coincidental and unintended. Exception: the main character, Jesse Thompson, is a real, living person who has granted me permission to use his name in this work. He is not, nor has he any connection to the agencies forming the basis of this story.

Author's Notes

The Cold War was a state of political and military tension between the United States of America (Western Bloc) and the Soviet Union (Eastern Bloc) that took place from 1945 to 1991. Prior to the United States use of nuclear weapons against Japan in 1945, the Soviet Union had been developing technology to make similar devices. This gave rise to heightened espionage activities by both superpowers focusing on trying to gain advantage over the other in the areas specifically relating to their atomic weapons and defensive counter-measures preparedness. The extent of Soviet espionage and recruitment became evident with the notable defection to the Canadian government to Igor Gouzenko in 1946. It was during this period that the Canadian government also formed the alliances known as NATO (North Atlantic Treaty Organization) and NORAD (North American Air Defence Command), and included a joint partnership with the Americans in the construction and manning of the DEW Line: the early warning radar network in Canada's high north against a possible Soviet missile attack from over the North Pole. In addition to this, The Royal Canadian Navy, which was considered, at the time, the leader in the development of ASW – anti-submarine warfare technologies and ship launched air attack systems. I have drawn upon the available released historical records and background materials in the writing of this work of fiction. These references are readily available in the public domain (Internet) and in public and military archives.

The Halifax Incident

A Jesse Thompson Cold War Suspense

H. Paul Doucette

Print ISBNs
Amazon print 9780228633631
Ingram Spark 9780228633648
BWL Print 9780228633655

BWL Publishing Inc.

Books we love to write ...
Authors around the world.

http://bwlpublishing.ca

Copyright 2024 by H. Paul Doucette
Editor Nancy M. Bell
Cover artist Pandora Designs

Table of Contents

Prologue

March, 10, 1959, 10:30 pm The Lord Elgin Hotel, Ottawa
Josef Sokolov

Josef Sokolov sat in the thick upholstered chair, listening to the music playing on the radio with his eyes closed. It was one of the few indulgences of western capitalist culture he enjoyed. He held a cut crystal glass containing clear vodka in one hand; his forearm resting on the arm of the chair while moving the other hand in time with the music like a baton.

The Lord Elgin Hotel was frequently used by the Soviet Embassy staff for discrete meetings with various agents and other people away from the embassy. This was because the embassy was under constant surveillance by the RCMP, Canada's security service, and by the GRU. The Soviet Military Intelligence Organization maintained vigilant surveillance over everyone inside the building and were responsible for all espionage activities outside of the Soviet Union.

A sharp rap on the door of the room shattered Sokolov's reverie, causing him to open his eyes. The door opened and Sergie Agapov walked in. He wore a three-piece suit and a hat; he carried a black leather valise in his hand.

Agapov was a member of the Soviet delegation posted to the embassy in Ottawa as an attaché in the Trade Office. In truth, he was actually an agent with the GRU, and Sokolov's handler. He was a dedicated and loyal party member with aspirations of advancement to loftier positions within the Politburo. Agapov arrived at the embassy in nineteen-fifty-seven, two years ago, taking the post he now held.

Josef Sokolov knew this about him and harboured a healthy mistrust of the man. He hated the GRU, equating them on the same level as the old Gestapo, only more sinister and brutal.

Both men were graduates from the Military University in Moscow, however, Sokolov had entered into service in the Komitet Gosudarstvennoy Bezopasnosti, or KGB. His first assignment was to establish himself in Canada using the cover of a chef with Belgium papers. His reason for coming to Canada: to open a restaurant with his wife. The plan was to open a place catering to government politicians and government workers where they could listen in on discussions through well placed 'bugs', the infamous listening devices. Within two years their ploy began to work, yielding a number of useful intelligence reports.

They had been working together for the last eight months and they learned of Agapov's underhanded methods when dealing with the agents under his control; spying on them, taking credit for their successes and reporting any grievances to their superiors through innuendo and gossip. Then there was the matter of the relationship with his partner and paramour, Ivanka Chenko. He suspected for some time now that Agapov had his eye set on her.

"Interesting choice in music, Comrade?" Agapov said, looking at the radio as he came over and sat down on the matching chair opposite him, setting the valise and his hat on the small table. He picked up the other glass, also containing vodka which Sokolov had poured earlier.

"I like American jazz music," Sokolov said with a shrug and slight tilt of his head. "Is this why I am here, Comrade Agapov? To discuss my taste in music?"

The slight hint of disdain was not lost on Agapov, but he contained his annoyance. He knew from the beginning that Sokolov did not like him.

"You are here to receive your new assignment and orders," Agapov said tersely.

"I assumed as much. And they are what?"

"Moscow has recently learned the American Navy, along with the Canadian

Navy, have developed some new means of detecting submarine traffic, notably, nuclear submarines. Our agents in America have reported this project, code-named, SOSUS, which is being deployed on the ocean floor. If they have found a way to monitor submarine movements then it is imperative we find out, and quickly. I have been in contact with my counterpart in Washington and he reports that this new system may actually already be in place. However, he cannot confirm this, since his operation is under suspicion from the FBI."

"Uh-huh."

"Can you turn off that music? It is distracting," Agapov said, testily.

Sokolov slowly stood up, went to the radio and turned it off.

"Better, spasiba," he said, as Sokolov sat back down.

"As I was saying, this means any attempt to penetrate their security would likely prove highly dangerous and costly. So, you will try to get what we need from the Canadian side."

"And just where do I start?"

"We have learned that much of the Canadian Navy's participation appears to be at a location in Halifax, Nova Scotia at a base called, HMCS Stadacona and at the Naval Research Establishment that is also located there. Their Atlantic Fleet is based and operates from the port. According to the reports from our agents, this new system involves the Canadians at a place called

Shelburne. It is apparently posing as a oceanographic research facility, as near as we have been able to ascertain. You will go to Halifax; I assume your contact there is still active?"

Sokolov sat quietly, looking into his glass for a moment considering his orders.

"As far as I know, yes. Although, I have not been in contact with him for a few months," he finally said, looking up.

"Why not?"

"No reason to. I was re-assigned to another task, as you well know."

"Can he be trusted to cooperate with you again?"

"Probably. He is a believer; a loyal Communist."

"You will make contact with him and obtain whatever you can on this operation, then proceed there and get the information."

"Just like that," Sokolov said, snapping his fingers in the air. "Does Moscow think I can just walk onto their bases and ask to see everything?"

"You are the master spy," Agapov said, reaching for the bottle of vodka. "You will figure out a way." It was his turn to inflect a hint of sarcasm. "We know that much of the research in ASW technology is being done here in Ottawa by their National Research Council, and at other facilities. However, as I said a moment ago, Moscow believes the operation in question is being run from their base in Halifax through this naval research establishment group and seems to be independent from their other research locations."

"When do I go to Halifax?" Sokolov asked.

"As soon as you can make your arrangements."

"What am I looking for specifically?"

"If our information is correct, we will need to know exactly what this new system entails and any other related information, especially dealing with their development of a working sonar detection system and a new type of torpedo or depth charge that can be used from their aircraft, which would mean they could possibly track our submarines and attack them from the air. Our information is not clear on that point. You must obtain confirmation of this and, if true, copies of any relevant documents."

"And this information is reliable?"

"According to headquarters. The information was obtained from our station in Washington. This contact in Halifax, does he have access to what we need?"

"Yes, I think so. He is one of the electronics engineers working in radio wave theory."

"And you are sure he will work with you?" Agapov asked again.

"Yes. We identified him two years ago, before you arrived and cultivated him since then."

"We?" Agapov asked.

"Chenko and I."

"So...?"

"So, yes, she will be coming with me. We work as a team; our cover, remember?"

"This will have to be cleared with Moscow."

Sokolov sipped his drink and looked at him. 'Politics,' he thought, 'always politics.'

"We have no one there to monitor any operation," Agapov went on.

"You mean to spy on us," he said in a casual tone.

"You know the rules," Agapov snapped.

"How long? I have to make arrangements."

"I will call immediately. Where will you be?"

"Chenko's."

"Two hours then," Agapov said, standing up. "I see no problem getting the authority, so you can make your arrangements. You will of course, report in on a daily basis with progress reports."

"Of course," he said, standing as well.

A half hour later, he was sitting in the apartment he and Ivanka Chenko's shared; although she to those around them she known as Adela Maes. They met ten years earlier in Russia at a secret KGB training facility located one hundred kilometres outside of Leningrad near the Finnish border. Both graduated from the university with degrees which included acquiring fluency in English. They were immediately recruited into the KGB.

"When do we leave?" she asked after he finished his recounting his meeting with Agapov.

She was standing at the small stove tending to the dish cooking in the skillet. He liked watching her, which he did often. At thirty-two, she was a striking woman. She came from Ishim, a small township in the Chelyabinsk Oblast, or region. Her family were peasant farmers, some also worked in a local armaments factory. She was lucky to be born with a good mind and eventually came to the attention of the area political officer who promoted her to attend the university in Moscow when she came of age.

"In the next couple of days," he answered. "Agapov is awaiting approval from Moscow."

"I hate that man," she said without turning from the stove. "He's a pig."

"I know. I cannot move against him it would be too dangerous for you."

"I know," Ivanka said softly.

"Are you still of a mind to pursue what we talked about?"

"Yes."

Several months before, while on an assignment, they were targeted by the GRU internal security section for suspected crimes against the state. They discovered that a report had been submitted by Agapov's predecessor who had a running feud with Sokolov over some ridiculous issue. They were cleared, of course, but GRU had been suspicious of the couple ever since. The incident was sufficient enough that they began discussing the possibility of defecting to the west. But they both had large families back in Russia and retaliations were a definite concern. However, they did agree that, if a situation arose with the GRU which endangered them, they would make their escape.

She picked up a dish towel and took hold of the skillet. Turning, she stepped to the table and set it on a small place mat in the middle, then sat down. It contained a hot potato and corned beef concoction the locals called hash. They both liked it as it reminded them of home.

"I am thinking this assignment could be our opportunity," he said, holding up his plate. "We may not get another chance like this again. Besides, I think he's beginning to suspect something."

"I agree," she said, scooping out a spoonful of the fried hash. "You are sure he has not placed someone down there?"

"As far as I know from talking with Karl and Alexi, no one has been sent there."

There were other agents he was close to who were working in Ottawa and Toronto. Their community of spies was limited to six agents so any sudden re-assigning would be noticed.

"But it will still be very dangerous, yes?" she asked.

"Yes, but I believe the Canadian security presence in Halifax is minimal and mostly operated by their navy based there."

"So, no RCMP or military intelligence operatives?"

"Not so as to be a concern," he said, using his fork to pull a piece of the corned beef apart.

"Then who would we approach or contact?"

"I will figure that out."

She reached a hand over and placed it on his saying, "I trust you."

* * *

Sergei Agapov

Shortly after his meeting with Sokolov, Agapov returned to the embassy and once inside his office, picked up his phone and dialed four numbers.

"Da?" a man said after the second ring.

"Send Comrade Pavlo Palyvoda to my office," Agapov ordered, then hung up the phone.

Thirty-five minutes later there was a knock on his door.

"Enter," he said.

A tall, heavyset man in his forties stepped inside closing the door behind him.

16

"Comrade," Pavlo Palyvoda said, coming to attention in front of Agapov's desk. "You wanted to see me?"

"Da," Agapov said, looking the man over. Palyvoda had been recruited from Georgia; one of the Soviet Unions southern Oblasts.. He proved himself to be an utterly ruthless agent and enforcer, a lethal blunt instrument. He had been with KGB for the last ten years. Agapov had used him on past missions with satisfaction. Pavlova held a unique position with the KGB at the embassy. He operated outside the usual chains of command and was almost completely answerable to Agapov.

"Relax. I called you here for another assignment. Do you know comrades Sokolov and Chenko?"

"Da."

"And do they know you?"

"Not as far as I know, sir. As you know, I do not work in the embassy directly."

"Good. They have been given a sensitive assignment in Halifax, Nova Scotia. We do not have any agents in place there. I need you to go to Halifax and monitor their activities, reporting directly back to me."

"I understand," Palyoda said. "Is there something specific you are concerned about?"

"Let's just say that I have suspicions; nothing definite, but still...I sense something questionable is going on."

"And you want me to do what exactly?"

17

"For the moment, just observe and report. I will issue orders and instructions as warranted by their actions."

"Yes sir. When do I leave?"

"Tonight. Take this." He passed him a piece of paper with a single name, Caroline Simpson, and telephone number typed on it. "Memorize it then destroy it. Use it only if necessary."

Palyvoda nodded then turned away and headed for the door. Agapov watched him as he walked away. If they were planning something that threatened the Motherland Pavloda would be there to terminate them.

Chapter One

One week earlier ~ Jesse Thompson

It was just past three o'clock in the morning and I was sitting in a comfortable seat in first class in a Canadair CL44 on my way to Ottawa having just finished wrapping up a murder investigation in Tuktoyuktuk, Northwest Territories. The case involved the murder of a local Inuit fisherman who was reported missing by the detachment in Sach's Habour. I had been sent because the incident happened close to one of the DEW Line installations and there had been reports of possible Soviet submarine activity in the area.

I was being called back to Ottawa for re-assignment that sounded urgent. Lucky for me, I managed to get a flight on a 'Red Eye' out of Yellowknife. I knew one of the flight attendants who fixed it for me to take a seat in first class, since that section of the plane was mostly empty which suited me just fine. The usual travellers who would be in this section didn't fly this late at night. The only other people in the section with me were a pregnant woman with her husband and an older woman who seemed to be related to them.

Tonight, the main cabin area was half full. There were several nurses returning home from a tour in Frobisher Bay and eight liquored-up technicians, rotating out from twelve weeks at one of the DEW Line installations. They were obviously happy to be heading south. Twelve weeks working above the Arctic Circle was no picnic, especially in the winter months...I know. I kept an eye on them for a while from where I sat, but soon realized they were harmless and the two cabin attendants seemed to have everything in hand, so I tried to catch some nap time. The last thought I remember before I went to sleep was that of Marie Chaisson.

I finally arrived in Ottawa at ten in the morning to find a car waiting for me. Must be important I thought, as I climbed in back while the driver put my luggage in the trunk.

The first thing I saw when I entered Deputy Superintendent Marcus Warton's office was the beautiful face of Marie Chassion, his assistant, and the love of my life. The smile on her face washed away all sense of fatigue from my trip.

"Hello lover," she said with just enough of a hint of sensuality to send a shiver through me. "Go straight in, he's expecting you."

I stepped to her desk, dropped my bag, leaned in and kissed her on the lips.

"Mmmmmmm," she hummed when we parted. "Enough of that...get in there."

"Yes ma'am," I said, tossing her a curt salute.

"Come," Warton said from the other side of door after I knocked. I opened the door and went in, closing it again behind me.

Marcus Warton was a big boned and muscular man with a thick crop of snow-white hair and piercing clear blue eyes.

"Sir." I went to went to one of the chairs in front of his large wooden desk and sat down.

"Welcome back. How'd it go?" he asked once I was settled.

"A local Inuit fisherman was reported missing to the detachment in Tuktoyuktuk. His body, what was left of it, was spotted by a passing bush pilot. Looks like he was shot up pretty badly; same thing with his kayak."

"Not a local matter then?"

"I don't think so. Near as I was able to find out from the medical examiner in Yellowknife, the calibre of a round recovered from the body appears likely to have been from a Russian AK-47. I reported the matter to the security staff at the radar installation in Tuk so they could take steps. I think the area detachment can handle the police part."

"An AK-47, you say? So, it's the bloody Russians, again."

"Yeah, looks that way," I said. "They are really desperate to get anything on the DEW Line system."

"I assume you have written a report?"

"It's in my bag. I'll leave it with Marie when I leave."

"By the way, judging from the look of you it was a long flight."

"The 'Red Eye'," I answered. "It'll do that. I take it I'm not here for a hearty bon voyage when I head out for my long overdue leave?"

"Sorry, no," Warton said, leaning forward and sliding a brown file folder across the desktop toward me. I reached out and picked it up, opening it.

"Came in yesterday morning from the DSTI, the Directorate of Scientific and Technological Intelligence. You'll note the red 'Top Secret' stamp. Take a moment."

There were three pages inside the folder, each stamped top secret. The information contained in the report stated that they had received a confidential communique from the FBI's electronic surveillance section in Washington.

The section was responsible for monitoring all foreign communication traffic involving the Soviets. In this instance, they indicated traffic from Moscow over the last five days, specifically, between the GRU, the Soviet's military intelligence organization, and the KGB operations in the States. The Bureau's code breakers were able to unlock the messages and discovered a series of urgent orders to gather information on our anti-submarine warfare research and development programs as soon as possible.

When I finished reading the document four minutes later, I closed the folder and set it on the desk.

"What else is new," I said, "they've been after this information since the end of the last war," I said. "As I recall, they were spying on us when we were allies."

"True," Warton said, pulling the folder closer to him. "I think Churchill had it right when he said our next war would come from the east. Regardless, it's the use of the word urgency in the transmissions that is causing concerns down south. After all, they are somewhat invested in the work our navy is doing. Ever since Stalin exploded his atomic bomb, there has been a significant shift in defence thinking. Now it seems, everyone is looking to a naval solution since the DEW Line became operational. Their thinking is that the Soviets may be building a submarine adjunct as a countermeasure to the DEW Line. Hence, their sudden interest in the work in that area, notably in the development of ASW systems."

"I know. I see they didn't include their views on why the Soviets are placing this urgency for the information now. Don't they have agents on the ground in these locations?"

"Usually, yes, but military intelligence hasn't been able to confirm that."

"And you expect me to...what?"

He ignored the question, saying instead, "The navy has reached the testing stage and are fitting a prototype of the new system on one of the new St. Laurent class destroyer escorts at the Davies yard in Quebec in a month, and at the Halifax Shipyards in a week or ten days for sea trials."

"They think the Soviets have found this out and that's why the urgency?" I asked.

"We should proceed on the assumption they have, on the other hand, the Feds are not so sure, which is why we're talking. From this day forward, I am re-assigning you to look into this matter. As always, you will work under your own guidance as you see appropriate. I chose you because of your qualifications and the fact you speak fluent Russian. I need you to go to Quebec and Halifax to investigate and report back."

"Do we have any resources in either place I can draw on for back-up and location background?"

"Yes. Marie has prepared a packet for you with what you will need, including your travel arrangements and accommodations. By the way, I want you to make contact with a Dr. Karen Mitchell at the NRC, the Naval Research Council, here in Ottawa. Marie has already made the appointment for this afternoon. She's closely connected to the development of the new sonar systems and she also sits on the board at DSTI. Well, I think that about covers it. Good luck," he said, extending his hand across to me. I stood and grabbed it. "Oh, almost forgot. You can leave tomorrow at the latest." He gave me a knowing smile when added this. "You two have a good night."

He is one sly old fox.

"Thanks. We will."

Back in the outer office, Marie was holding up a large brown envelope and eyeing me with a suggestive grin.

"Your appointment is set for one o'clock; the address is on a piece of paper inside the envelope. Your travel papers are inside as well. I have already alerted the local DS at the headquarters depot in Halifax you'll be arriving, along with the local intelligence office. It's all in there."

I am always impressed by her efficiency...among her other assets.

"The boss is cutting me loose after lunch, so I'll be shopping for dinner, any preference?"

"Meat. Red meat," I said, smiling. "The rest I leave to you."

"Okay. You have some time before you meet Dr Mitchell, any plans?"

"Shower. Shave. Sleep. In that order."

"Good plan. You look like someone just out of the wilds."

"And I'll show you just how wild later," I said, bending down and giving her a long kiss on the lips.

Later, refreshed and with a clean change of clothes, I arrived at the office of Doctor Karen Mitchell. Marie had included a single sheet of paper listing Mitchell's credentials and a bit of background information.

Chapter Two

Jesse Thompson

Karen Mitchell received her Doctorate degree in Oceanography, specializing in acoustics and electronics, from Brown University in the States. Upon her return to Canada, she accepted a position with the National Research Council, then later, divided her time with the Naval Research Establishment to work on the sonar systems project because of her qualifications in acoustics. She also held a seat with the Directorate of Scientific and Technical Intelligence. A very impressive resume.

Her secretary escorted me into her office, introducing me.

"Inspector Thompson," she said, standing to the side. "Your one o'clock appointment."

She was an attractive well-dressed woman in her late forties, maybe early fifties. She was dressed in a two-piece outfit with a plain white blouse, business-like but still feminine with a slight hint of chic. She wore little make-up, again just enough to show her femininity.

"Inspector," Dr. Mitchell said as she stood up, extending her hand and gestured to a leather padded chair with her other hand. "Please."

"Jesse, please," I said, accepting her hand. I noted she had a soft and but firm grip; obviously sure and confident.

"Thank you. Karen. May I offer you a coffee or tea?" She sat back down.

"No thank you, I'm okay. Besides, I do not want to take too much of your time."

"I must say, I was a bit surprised when I received the call to tell me that I was to expect a visit from the RCMP intelligence office. I can only assume you probably know I am also connected with intelligence?"

"Yes. I was briefed on your various functions. The RCMP has been working closely with the intelligence communities here and in the States, most notably on the DEW Line, but also in several other areas of mutual interest, such as SOSUS."

"Interesting that the force would be so deeply active."

"Well, we are, more or less, Canada's national police agency with a mandate which includes internal security."

She sat looking at me and nodded.

"In that context," she began, "the FBI recently alerted us to possible KGB or GRU interest in certain projects that the navy is involved in with the Americans, specifically concerning your research into ASW and deterrence development. We know the

Soviets have taken an interest in what we are doing but have not been aware that they have actually taken steps to act directly against us."

"We're not sure they have," I said, "that's my job; to find out and if so, stop them."

"I see. What is it you think I can do?"

"In regards to my investigation? Nothing. What I need is a general overview of what specifically they would be looking for and where the information would be located."

"As to the work, suffice it to say, that it is of a highly technical nature so, unless you have an electronics engineering degree, whatever I tell you would sound like gibberish, no offence," she said with a hint of a smile and sounding sincere. "In regards to what the Soviets would want...in a nutshell; all of it. However, the good news is there simply is too much research material, so whatever they were to obtain would be fragmentary and as such, probably meaningless or require months, if not years, to put it together enough to see where we are going."

"What you say makes sense," I said. "Unfortunately, our experience with them has proved they are capable at getting enough to prove valuable. Where is most of the research being done?"

"At Stadacona, the naval base, and the NRE facilities in Dartmouth. The actual physical part of the program is being done at the Halifax Shipyards which is located next to HMC Dockyard; the other part of the navy's base."

"What is the security like at these locations?"

"Very good. The navy is responsible for overall security, however, they have a solid relationship with Army Intelligence and the local police. We liaise with the head of naval intelligence; a Lieutenant Commander Jules Swanson, I believe."

"The army is in Halifax?"

"Yes, mostly Reserves, consisting of infantry and signals companies. Oh, and there is a small armour, supply, and artillery element, as I understand it."

"I know of your connection with the DSTI; does this mean they have resources in Halifax?"

"Not directly, no. As I said, we keep abreast of what is going on through our connection with naval intelligence. It was decided to leave the security to the navy. Anything else?"

"Is it possible to get a copy of an overview of the projects? Something along the lines of what your group might pass to a politician on one of the committees running oversight."

She gave me a wry smile and I thought I caught just a flicker of amusement in her eyes.

"I think I have just the thing."

I stood up and extended my hand.

"Thanks for your help and time," I said, smiling at her. "It's been a pleasure."

"You're very welcome, and good hunting."

She released my hand and picked up her phone. Ten minutes later, I left her office with all the information I requested and headed for Marie's apartment.

* * *

Jesse Thompson

My plane touched down at the HMCS Naval Air Station in Dartmouth on the other side of Halifax Harbour at ten-thirty in the morning. It was an uneventful trip, departing Montreal on a direct flight to Nova Scotia. I had just finished my investigation in Quebec at the Davies Shipyard where part of the research on the new sonar systems was being carried out.

After several days I was satisfied the risk was unlikely to be here, so I booked a flight with the RCAF on one of their transport flights to Halifax. I always took advantage of military transport whenever possible, preferring the privacy afforded by the absence of civilian travellers. Marie had made arrangements to billet me in the Officer's Quarters at HMCS Stadacona.

When I de-planed, I was met by a corporal who said he had been ordered to drive me where I needed to go. I sensed Marie's handiwork...again. He took my travel bag and led me to a staff car parked by the hanger. He put the bag in the boot and I got in on the front passenger seat which caused him to give me a surprised look.

"I'm no one special," I said, as he slid in behind the wheel.

"Yes sir, if you say so," the junior NCO said, starting the engine.

The drive took forty minutes, which included a ride across the newly built Angus L. MacDonald Bridge or, as I was to learn, simply called the MacDonald, that actually crossed over HMC Dockyard, ending right at Stadacona.

I sat looking out the window at the city below. There were signs of new growth in what I took to be the downtown area which surrounded the old military fort situated on top of a high hill that the locals called, Citadel Hill, or simple the Citadel. Its real name was Fort George. I knew from what I read before leaving Ottawa, that it was being developed into a national park and museum. However, the most striking observation was the view of both the naval vessels in the dockyard and the open dry dock in the Halifax Shipyards. Specifically, the view of the destroyer escort ship sitting inside it. I automatically looked up, thinking there had to be some sort of monitoring device covering the pedestrian walks on either side of the roadway. There were none.

Once on the base, the driver dropped me at the officer's quarters where I had been assigned a room to myself. When I signed in, the duty clerk; a young fresh-faced kid wearing the traditional black sailor's uniform: a jumper with flap that hung down the back from the shoulders and bell bottom pants, passed me a sealed envelope, stamped CONFIDENTIAL and my room key.

He gave me instructions to where my room was located, and I thanked him. It was nearly four-thirty when I finally got squared away in the room. By the time I unpacked, I realized just how tired I was and all I wanted was a meal, a shower and then bed, in that order. I decided to take advantage of the mess for dinner then call it a day.

I rose early the next morning as was my custom, feeling better and rested. I quickly dressed for my routine run before breakfast; usually about two miles. I remembered reading that the MacDonald bridge was just under a mile, so an easy run across and back over the span would suffice and gave me an opportunity to confirm a suspicion I had from yesterday.

On the return run, I slowed and carefully looked over the scene below.

I had a clear view of all the ships tied alongside, including their equipment – radar, RDF antennae and armaments. I also had a clear view of the shipyards to the north, noting the destroyer that was currently in dry dock. I reckoned it had to be the one being outfitted with the new ASW technology. As I neared the end of the bridge, I couldn't help thinking how easy it would be to photograph everything since there was nothing to prevent it.

Back in my room, I showered and shaved then dressed in my civilian clothes and strapped on my shoulder holster with my service revolver tucked under my arm. After a quick check in the mirror, I headed downstairs for breakfast.

Later, back in my room, I took out the information sheet Marie had prepared with names and phone numbers on it. I picked up the phone and, after connecting with an outside line, dialed the number for the RCMP Headquarters here in the city. When I reached the duty officer, I set up an appointment with the Unit Commander; his name was Inspector Bryon McKinnon. The meeting was set for ten o'clock. Before hanging up, I asked if he could begin making arrangements for me to sign out an unmarked car.

I was told the inspector would expect me at 10 am. I told the clerk I would be right down. I took a cab from the base down to the headquarters building at 203 Hollis Street.

The building was located in a part of the city that was a stark mix of new buildings that were erected amid remnants of the city's past. In some ways it felt like stepping back into the nineteenth century.

The headquarters building, like that of Province House, the provincial seat of government, across the street was built in the old European Georgian style. A three story red stone structure with banks of high windows along its main face, fronting Cheapside Lane. It always surprises me how many places in this country still cling to the architecture of the old country and the last century, even down to adorning the buildings with classical sculptures such as the one on the roof; an amazon riding a chariot. Our colonial roots ran deep.

When I entered the main reception area and presented myself to the duty officer, he directed me to the second floor where McKinnon's office was located.

Inspector Bryon McKinnon was a twenty year veteran of the force with a background in criminal investigation and, for the last three years, as an intelligence officer in the intelligence section. According to the briefing I had on him, he was assigned here as part of a joint intelligence program overseeing the ASW development the navy was engaged in and the US SOSUS project down in Shelburne.

I knocked on the wooden door.

"Come," a voice said from the other side.

I opened the door and stepped in, closing it behind me.

"Inspector Thompson, I presume?" McKinnon said, standing up and offering an outstretched hand which I accepted once I stood in front of his desk.

"That's right," I said, "and it's Jesse."

"Good to meet you. It's Byron." He had a firm grip. "Sit. Get you a coffee? Tea?"

"No, thanks. I'm good." I sat on one of the wooden chairs in front of the desk.

"I received a call from your boss, Deputy Superintend Warton yesterday, alerting me of your arrival and the reason behind your visit. According to him, the FBI has been in touch with our Intelligence people in Ottawa concerning information they obtained about a possible KGB operation that may be targeting us here. I must confess, I was more than a little surprised that we were not contacted right away."

"Probably because the alert wasn't sent directly to us. The contact was first made to the DSTI who then passed it along to the rest of us. I was brought in on this myself at the last minute, so to speak."

I could see he was a bit miffed and wanted to let him know my being here had nothing to do with him or his operations.

"Ever since that business with Igor Gouzenko back in forty-six, everyone's been stepping carefully whenever the KGB is mentioned. So it didn't come as much of a surprise to us when we were asked to look into the allegation."

"All the same, this poses a serious issue for us here. This command really isn't set up to deal with actual KGB agents running around. Our role here is to support naval intelligence when needed. Mostly background checks on personnel and random spot checks at the various facilities. We also undertake investigations and apprehension of foreign agents, although up to now that hasn't been an issue. Warton told me that you've been dealing with them up north?"

"That's right," I said. "Mostly in connection with the DEW Line installations. The Soviets have increased their submarine operations in the Arctic lately. I figure the brass thinks my background would help deal with this supposed threat, so I'm here to investigate and, hopefully, identify any threats and shut them down."

He gave me a funny look when I said this, perhaps not so much funny as concerned.

"Not to worry," I said. "I don't usually have to use violence as a general rule."

"Right," he said with a hint of relief in his voice. "How can I help? I have been ordered to give whatever assistance you require."

"I suppose the first thing I need to know is how the security at the naval base is handled?"

"It's pretty much the same as it was during the war, though significantly reduced, but they have kept up with the obvious changes that have come with the times. By and large, it has been pretty good and well managed, so far."

"What about the shipyard? I noticed it was connected to the dockyard when I crossed the MacDonald Bridge yesterday."

"They are a private company, so any internal security is probably private, although, whenever one of the navy's ships is in for maintenance or re-fitting, the navy has their own people in place and sensitive documents are never kept there, except when needed when a ship is dry docked."

"Like now."

"Pardon?"

"I saw a ship in the dry dock. I assume it's one of the new destroyer escorts in for fitting out the new ASW systems?"

"You know about that?" he said. "Of course, you would. Yes, especially in this instance. I was made aware of what they were going to do and was included to provide assistance, if warranted, but it is strictly a navy operation."

"I couldn't help noticing that there is nothing to prevent anyone from photographing whatever was being done from the bridge. The ships below are all completely open to view, even in the dry dock. Don't they see this as a concern?"

"I can't answer that question; those areas are under the navy's control. Perhaps you should pay them a visit and ask them."

"Thanks, I think I will. I don't suppose you can point me to the person I should talk to?"

"Lieutenant Commander Jules Swanson, my counterpart, so to speak; he is recently arrived from England; Royal Navy. I'll call ahead and alert him you are coming. Anything else?"

"HMCS Shelburne?"

"We are kept in the loop, but as I have said, strictly a navy operation. Our connection to what they are doing down there is through the Naval Research Establishment and the DSTI in a support role. They keep us posted, but that's about it. I'll make the call now."

Five minutes later, my meeting with Swanson was set for eleven-thirty. McKinnon and I stood and shook hands. I told him I looked forward to working with him and if it was okay I would like to arrange for a desk here at headquarters. He said it would arranged.

I stopped at the duty desk on my way out and asked if the car I requested was available. It was and, after signing for it, the clerk passed over the keys with directions to where it was parked. I thanked him and headed outside. The car, a nondescript black four door Ford sedan, was parked on Bedford Row; once inside, I took off back to Stadacona and my meeting with Lieutenant Commander Jules Swanson.

Chapter Three

Josef Sokolov

The day promised to be relatively warm and comfortable for March. The city still had traces of snow on the ground; small dirty snowbanks running along the curbs. But the driving and walking were easy, as evidenced by the traffic busily going about its business.

Josef Sokolov stood at the window of the room scanning the street outside, eyeing the people walking along the sidewalk. Men and women; mostly women, moving past each other as they headed their business. He also noted the number of uniformed sailors among the crowd. He found himself thinking of Moscow and the distinct differences between the two cities: each a world apart.

He and Ivanka Chenko arrived in the city two days earlier and, after taking rooms at the Waverley Inn, he immediately made contact with his source; a man named Peter Wilcox and completed arrangements to meet. He also asked Wilcox to bring anything he could on the work he was doing.

Western campuses had proved to be rich fields for recruitment with many of these future graduates assuming important positions in business and government; a valuable lesson learned at Cambridge and Oxford Universities in England.

Wilcox was born in nineteen-thirty to a middle-class couple as an only child. He attended school and then finished a Bachelor of Science degree from Dalhousie University, one of the local universities, with a minor in Political Science. After graduation, he enrolled in a four year diploma program at the Nova Scotia Technical College, graduating with a diploma in electronics, specializing in radio wave theory.

It was while pursuing his minor; Political Science, that he was introduced to the great European political thinkers including Karl Marx and Friedrich Engels and their ideas of Socialism and Communism. It was a fated match and he quietly delved deeper into this area of political thought, eventually adopting their philosophy as his own. However, he soon realized that if he wanted to obtain government employment in his field, he would have to maintain a very low and discrete profile to avoid coming to the attention of the country's intelligence services.

Sokolov met and recruited him several years earlier while on an assignment to investigate the possibility of recruiting local assets. It was not long after their initial meeting that he informed Wilcox he was

Russian and a communist. Wilcox was immediately interested in him and wanted to get to know him better and more about his political leanings. This evolved into several meetings where they discussed a number of issues. It was at their fourth meeting that Sokolov recruited him to assist in furthering the Soviet cause by working with him and providing him with information. Since then, Wilcox had been a reliable source of important information on the developments in such areas as the navy's work on a new type of torpedo that would be deployed from an aircraft and work being done on a new sonar system.

Wilcox proposed they should meet in the railroad station; it had a small lunch counter, and they would be less conspicuous there than elsewhere. Sokolov agreed, thinking it was as good a place as any to meet and it was close to the Waverley Inn. The meeting was arranged for two o'clock.

Sokolov checked his watch: it read one-forty; plenty of time. He stepped away from the window and crossed the room and picked up his overcoat and hat.

"I am leaving now for my meeting," he said to Ivanka, who was stretched out on the bed reading the paper.

"*Shasleeva*," she said, wishing him 'good luck' as she looked over the top of the paper.

He left and headed for the street. Ten minutes later he stood in front of the rail station. There were several dozen people milling about the area, some with luggage, some looking around, obviously there to meet an arrival. He went to the glass panelled doors and went inside.

The first thing he encountered was the noise: the cacophony of multiple voices all speaking at the same time mingled with metallic sounding announcements from the overhead speakers, calling out arrivals and departures.

The main terminal was actually small as rail stations go, he thought, standing among the densely packed press of people. It was wide open with a high roof and rows of wooden benches filling the central floor area. Ticket and baggage sections were on the right as you came in; both had lines in front of them. He spotted the lunch counter down at the far end on the left side of the room.

He eased his way through the mob of people towards it. When he reached the counter, he made his way to the end where he found an empty table with three chairs. He took one, signalling for the waitress to bring him a coffee.

Ten minutes later, he spotted Wilcox making his way towards him, looking agitated and nervous.

"Why so nervous, Comrade," Sokolov said softly, when Wilcox reached the table.

"Just being careful," Wilcox answered, taking a seat.

"Why? Has something happened?"

"There was a visit from the RCMP yesterday. They said it was a routine spot check they did at all the research facilities."

Sokolov knew the Royal Canadian Mounted Police was part of the national intelligence community, operating in cooperation with their counterparts in the military here in Canada and in the United States.

"So? Did they say what they were looking into?"

"No, but at a guess, I'd say it has something to do with the upcoming trials of the new sonar system."

"On that point, have you been able to obtain any information?"

"Not yet. Security around it is unusually tight this time."

"Do you know when and where the trial is to take place?'

"All I know so far, is the physical component is here and at the shipyard to be installed on a ship, probably a destroyer; one of the new class destroyer escorts."

"We need to see the research data."

"I understand," Wilcox said. "My problem is I don't know if the materials you need are here."

"Where is the information kept?" Sokolov asked.

"In a secure room at NRE. I think there are some documents in the records room at Stadacona, though I'm not positive."

"Do your best to find out, but be careful," Sokolov said. "What do you know about something named, SOSUS?"

"SOSUS? Not a lot. It's a project developed by the Americans involving fixed undersea devices, something to do with sound, I think. My department has been contacted on a couple of occasions to provide technical data and the mathematics of radio and sound waves through water, notably saltwater. Why?"

"We have recently learned of this and want to know more. Why is the Canadian Navy involved?"

"I don't know. That information is beyond my clearance level. Although I have heard it mentioned that whatever the reason, it has something to with an oceanographic research facility down in Shelburne."

"Hmmm. I see."

"I may know someone who might know more about it. She works at the Oceanography Institute in Dartmouth. I'll contact her."

"Carefully, always with care, da?"

"Always."

The KGB was aware that the Americans may have developed some sort of undersea listening system stretching all along the eastern and western seaboards of North America, possibly as far as Iceland, but Moscow seemed to not be indicating any interest.

"Do you think she would be interested in working for us?"

"I'll check. There were a few other students I met at university and at the tech college who felt as I did. She was one. I seem to recall one or two others who were recruited by the Russian government to work for them."

"Do that and get back to me as soon as you know. Do not contact them though, at least not before we talk again."

"Okay," Wilcox said. "That it? I really should be getting back."

"For now, and Comrade...thank you," Sokolov said, standing.

Wilcox stood as well, and the two men shook hands.

Sokolov watched the young man as he headed for the exit from the terminal. He left five minutes later, deciding to take a walk and consider his next moves with or without any information from Wilcox.

This situation with Shelburne presented a new set of concerns since the KGB believed that the information was here in Halifax. If it was actually located at another location, his mission was all but over. After all, he thought, how could he obtain what he needed without any resources to draw on? But it was not a complete washout. Wilcox could still be useful. According to him, the navy was about to install the new systems on a destroyer for trials. Perhaps there was something there he could get hold of to deliver to the Soviet scientists.

A half hour later, he returned to the Inn.

Ivanka was sitting on the sofa reading a book and listening to the radio when he entered the spacious, well-appointed room; the radio was tuned in to a local station, playing the latest popular music.

He went over to her and bent down, kissing the top of her head.

"Any word from Ottawa?" he asked.

"*Nyet*. Nothing. However, when I went out for some air, the clerk on the front desk stopped me to say someone had been in asking after us. He did not say who it was, only that it was a man."

"Curious," Sokolov said as he went and poured a glass of ice water.

"Agagov?"

"Most likely. After all, the embassy has no agents here. He made a comment about that fact before we left."

"Should we worry, you think?" she asked.

"Not yet," he answered, sitting on the sofa beside her. "If it becomes a problem, I will deal with it."

"How did your meeting go with Wilcox?"

"He is still loyal to the party ideals which surprised me. I suppose it must be the case with those who have never been to Russia. A shame. If they only knew; our work would be so much harder."

"You are becoming a cynic," she said with a wry smile.

"And you are not?" he said, smiling back.

"So, what will you do now? Agapov will expect something."

"I know. I will come up with something in the next day or two. Wilcox is looking into something that might help. In the meantime, I will have a look around, perhaps see what there is to learn about the security in the port."

"I can look into places like the YWCA or perhaps a military wives club. These bourgeois women do enjoy their bridge clubs and the like, maybe I can get into one."

"Good idea," he said, standing up. "Get your coat."

"Why? We going somewhere?"

"It is a nice day and I thought a walk would be enjoyable, then dinner at one of the local restaurants."

"Sounds wonderful. I will be just a few moments to freshen up."

She got up and headed for the bathroom, emerging ten minutes later looking radiant; much to his delight.

Later, as they walked down Barrington Street arm in arm, they were unaware of the man in a dark overcoat and snap brim fedora on the other side of the street. He was over a half block behind them and made sure to keep to where the most people were walking together.

Before the Russian couple left Ottawa, they took time to study a city map of Halifax the embassy had in their files, and because Sokolov had a photographic memory, he knew pretty much everything about the city, especially the various military facilities located there.

They proceeded down the street, looking like every other couple out walking. When they reached the corner of Buckingham Street, they stopped and looked up at the new bridge spanning the harbour.

"Let's walk up there," Sokolov said, gesturing with his head to the bridge.

"Why?" she asked as they continued walking.

"Believe it or not, the bridge actually crosses over their naval yard and has a completely unobstructed view of the shipyards connected at the north end with no apparent security measures."

"You have to love these Canadians," she said with just a hint of sarcasm.

"Do you still carry the mini-camera?"

She patted he small handbag.

"Excellent."

Twenty-five minutes later, they walked casually along the pedestrian walkway on the bridge. About a third of the way onto the bridge they stopped, seemingly admiring the view of the harbour. In reality, Ivanka had slipped the miniature camera from her handbag and was surreptitiously taking photographs of the ships below. Five minutes later, they crossed over to the opposite side and she repeated the action; this time including the dry dock at the shipyard and the navy ship inside it. Satisfied, they turned and headed back to the street at the Halifax end.

"What do you make of that covered section on that ship?" she asked, speaking in Russian since no one was close enough to hear her.

"I do not know. I will ask Wilcox the next time we meet. Although, it could be related to what we have been sent here to get. We will see. Now...dinner."

At about the same time, Pete Wilcox passed through the security gate at Stadacona, showing his identity card to the sailor on guard duty. He drove his '54 Triumph TR2 down to the parking area outside the building where he worked. It was the only 'splashy' item in his otherwise drab life

He found an empty spot, parked and got out. He climbed the four stone steps and went inside where he was met by another armed guard. He showed his card again even though he was well known to the security people.

His office was on the second floor, but he headed up to the top floor, one level up. That was where the records and file room was located. It was a highly secure area but because of the work he was engaged on, he had clearance to go inside. It contained four rows of dark grey steel file cabinets arranged along the full length of the room with two large wooden tables and four chairs at each end of the rows. Two rows of florescent lights provided plenty of light in addition to the three large windows in the facing wall.

A young WAVE rating sat at a small desk as he entered. Her name was Phyllis Roy. She was an attractive twenty-five-year-old woman with a clear, bright complexion and ash-blond hair. Standing at five-foot-four, she had a slim figure and the legs of a dancer.

She was responsible for the filing and making sure everyone entering was cleared and signed the logbook on the desktop.

"Hi, Phyllis," Wilcox said, bending over the logbook and picking up the pen. "How're you doing?"

"Hi. Okay," she said with a smile. "What are you after this time?"

He liked her and had taken her out to the movies on a couple of occasions.

"The usual, Need to double-check some notes and numbers."

"Okay. You know where to go. By the way, thanks again for the other night. I really wanted to see that movie, but not on my own."

"No problem. I really liked it too and it is always nice to spend time with you."

"You're sweet, thanks," she said with a hint of a blush rising in her cheeks.

"We'll hafta do it again," he said, standing upright, laying the pen along the crease of the book.

"I'd like that."

He smiled at her then moved off to the right in search of the cabinet with his files. When he reached the end of the row, he stole a quick glance back at her. She was busy going through sheets of paper to be filed later. He quietly stepped past his files in the second row of cabinets, and turned between the third and fourth rows. This was where some the records and files from Shelburne were kept.

He slowly moved down the aisle scanning the name tags in the front of each drawer looking for the one he wanted. He was about halfway down when he heard Phyllis call out his name and quickly dashed back to the end of the row. He managed to reach the table moments before she appeared.

"Oh, there you are," she said. "I was wondering, if you're free this Sunday, I would really like to cook dinner for you, maybe a roast chicken?"

"Sounds great," he said, waiting for his heart rate to slow down, hoping his voice didn't betray him. "Maybe we could go for drive before dinner, say down along the coast, or to Peggy's Cove, or Lawrencetown Beach? Weather permitting."

"Ooo, that sounds wonderful. So, it's a date then?"

"It's a date. I'll pick you up at, say one o'clock?" Good, he thought, she didn't see him in the wrong section.

"That'd be perfect. It'll give me time to start the chicken in the oven and change out of my church clothes."

One of these days he would have to do something about her, he thought when he looked at her, but not yet; he would bide his time. He liked her and she him, however, she was a devote Catholic, so no quick jump into the sack with this one.

Chapter Four

Jesse Thompson

I reached the main gate security hut leading onto the base, I stopped and pulled out my ID card. A navy rating wearing white webbing approached and bent down to eye the card. After a moment, he looked up at me and asked what my business was on the base. I told him I was billeted in the officer's quarters. He went inside the gatehouse and looked over some papers, then returned. He was about to wave me through when I asked him for directions to Lieutenant Commander Swanson's office which he gave me. I eased the car into gear then slowly went looking for the building and a parking spot.

The buildings and sheds were typical of military facilities in Canada, that is to say; austere, functional, and old. It was pretty much the same as it was during the last war, maybe even as far back as the first one. It was quite small for a major naval facility, so finding the building where Swanson's office was located proved simple enough. I parked in front of the building and got out. It was a three story stone structure with long rows of high windows running across the front.

Inside, I was met by yet another rating, this one was sitting at a reception desk. I showed him my card and asked where Swanson's office was located. He directed me to the third floor, room twelve. I thanked him and headed for the stairs; I assumed he was calling ahead to give him a heads up.

Lieutenant Commander Jules Swanson occupied a large double office at the end of the hall. Sitting in the outer office was a pretty WAVE dressed in the traditional black uniform of the navy. I noted the two red chevrons and anchor on her sleeve indicating her rank.

"Yes?" she said, looking up when I stepped inside.

"Inspector Thompson, RCMP Intelligence. I'm here to see the lieutenant commander. I believe he's expecting me," I said, stopping in front of her desk.

"Oh yes. Captain Waterman called. One moment, please," she said, reaching for her phone and dialing three numbers. After a moment, she said into the mouthpiece, "Inspector Thompson is here...yes sir."

"Go on in," she said with a cute smile, gesturing to the closed door.

"Thank you."

"Ah, Inspector," the fortyish man behind a dark mahogany desk said in a very British accent, as he stood up.

He was tall with thinning hair that was starting to show traces of grey at the temples. He sported a David Niven moustache under his long thin nose. He was almost a caricature of the British elite that you sometimes saw in American magazines. But it was his eyes that caught your attention: clear blue, bright, alert; leaving you feeling he was always watching everything around him.

"Thank you for taking this meeting. I know you must be busy," I said, taking a chair in front of the desk.

"Happy to oblige. I received a message of your arrival; something about a possible KGB operation or other coming our way."

"Something like that, yes. I've been sent down here to look into it."

"Well, our Red cousins have been eager to obtain as much intelligence as they can. One could be forgiven in thinking they do not have their own capabilities, so they have to steal other's work. Been that way almost from the beginning of Stalin's rise to power."

"True enough. I've been sent here to stop them. My job is to look into the possibility of collaborators, or people that can be identified as potential subjects open to exploitation by the Soviets."

"You mean blackmail?"

"That's right. It's one of the KGB's best tools they use on a regular basis."

"I can assure you that if they do come they will not find it so easy to gain access to any of the facilities currently working on these projects."

"That may be as you say, however, they have other means to get what they're after as I just indicated. Can you tell me how the people working on the sonar and other projects are vetted?"

"I see your point. In answer to your question, that's done, in part, by your people in collaboration with military intelligence and sometimes, the local police."

"Just how deep do they look?"

"Oddly, it seems that depends on the position being applied for, at least here."

"So, there is no standard practice? Procedure?"

"Oh, there is definitely a standard practice and procedure, to be sure, however, the extent of their screening is contingent on their required level of security clearance."

"And no one has spotted the flaw in that approach?"

"Flaw? How so?" he asked, looking interested.

"Say someone passes into a low-level position at, say the NRE, or here on the base, wouldn't they be working in the same departments as someone with a higher clearance? Following me?"

"Yes, I think I see where this is leading. However, there are safeguards and measures in place at these facilities, restricting access to sensitive areas to only those cleared to be there."

"But, I'm thinking it's still possible for someone to access those areas."

"Well, as they say, nothing is ever impossible, if you are clever enough. Although, I see no reason to try and steal sensitive or secret information unless you have someone or someplace to pass it to; you agree?"

I nodded, saying, "Good point. Then that leaves only one option; if someone is working here with possible ties to the Soviets, or with sympathies for their system, then he, or she, must have a contact. Which brings me back to my earlier question about your vetting procedures."

"So, what do you suggest," he asked.

"I assume that the number of people cleared to actually work on these projects directly are not that many?"

"As a matter of fact, you are correct. All in all, I would have to say there are not more than a dozen or so with high enough clearance to have access to the actual work being done at any level."

"Then, if you can arrange it, I would like to take a look at their personnel files and any attachments."

"That can be arranged. When would you like to begin?"

"Now's as good a time as any," I said.

"I am aware of your security clearance, so I will make the arrangements. Do you need any assistance?"

"Not just at the moment, thanks."

58

He reached for the phone and dialed.

"Susan, will you contact Smith over at the records office and let him know to expect a visit from Inspector Thompson. He is also to grant him access to any files he requests. Thank you."

"I will keep you posted on anything I may discover," I said, standing up. "If it is okay with you, I would like to keep an open channel to you on my investigation?"

"That is completely acceptable, thank you."

"Good, if something does come to light, we can coordinate a plan of action to deal with it."

"Agreed." He stood up and we shook hands.

"Susan will give you directions to the records department. A Lieutenant Walter Smith will meet you. Good luck."

I thanked him again then went back to the outer office where his assistant gave me directions to the records department which was here in this building.

Lieutenant Walter Smith met me when I stepped inside the large windowless room. A long counter ran the breadth of the room with an electrically operated gate at one end. Behind the counter there were two desks; one was obviously his, at the other about ten feet away, sat a navy rating wearing three red chevrons under a single foul anchor on his sleeve, indicating he was a leading seaman with three years good conduct and a trades patch on the other, a page and quill.

"Inspector Thompson?" Smith said, stepping up to the counter. "How can I help you? Lieutenant Commander Swanson has instructed me to provide you access to whatever you need."

He was a young man, maybe mid-late twenties, good looking with a friendly face.

"Thanks," I said. "Two things. I want to see all the personnel files of the people working on the NRE projects with clearance of Secret and higher, both civilian and military; and a quiet place to work."

He found me a small wooden table in one of the corners and I got ready for a long afternoon of reading files. He instructed the PO to get me a coffee and begin pulling the files. Fortunately, there were, as Swanson indicated, only a dozen files: seven civilians and five servicemen.

Two cups of coffee later, at four-twenty, I narrowed my search down to three files – two civilians and one army officer. By now, I was feeling a bit wired from the caffeine, and hungry. I asked Lieutenant Smith if it would be okay to take these files out of the department. He was reluctant at first, but when I pointed out that I billeted in the officer's quarters on base and had the security clearance, he agreed, insisting I sign the official logbook, noting the names of the files.

Back in my room and a full belly later, I sat at the writing desk and began to study the three files I took more careful look, starting with the army officer. I was a bit surprised that there were not more military personnel working on the projects since the end result was for their use. I also noted that everyone I looked at was a Canadian: no Americans.

Pulling out a notepad from one of the drawers, I began writing a profile on each one.

Name: Jerome Carew

Captain with Royal Canadian Corps of Engineers–eighteen years; single,

MSc mechanical and electrically engineering from Carleton University

Political affiliations; Progressive Conservative

Affiliations: Knights of Columbus, YMCA, Kinsmen, Halifax Club

Lives in officer's quarters in private residence in city

Reason for interest

Preliminary investigation uncovered possible memberships in certain

'gentleman's' clubs frequented by prominent local citizens-no known female

companions, possible alternate sexual orientation?

Name: Kevin Stewart

thirty-six years old; married, two children one, a boy, born

with a serious kidney defect.

BSc from Dalhousie University + Diploma NS Technical College
specialization: radio wave/acoustic engineering
No known political affiliations
Reason for interest
Risk of recruitment through his son

Name: Peter Wilcox
BSc + Diploma in electronics radio wave/acoustics from Dalhousie
and NS Tech
Background check uncovered a brief contact with a campus political group as
an undergrad–claims his reason was an interest in a girl who was an active
member; further investigation revealed that group was pro-soviet
Reason for interest:
Possibility may still be involved and pro-Soviet

All three were cleared by initial military intelligence background checks as well as a local police record check.

I knew from past experience that blackmail and coercion were two major methods used by Soviet agents when operating aboard and were always on the lookout for people they could convert or coerce to their cause; particularly those with something in their lives that they could use to their advantage.

In the case of the three people on my list there was a possible homosexual connection, which would ruin his career; an unhealthy child whose life was at risk, and a possible sympathizer.

The next morning, I arranged to meet with Swanson to go over my concerns.

I walked across the base to Swanson's office, arriving at about ten o'clock.

"Coffee?" he asked, when his orderly saw me into his office.

"Thanks; black," I said, taking the same chair as yesterday.

He nodded to the man behind me. "You say that you have spotted three possible risks?"

"I don't know to what degree they're a risk exactly, but yes, I think these people need another look." I passed him the personnel files along with the notes I wrote last night. "You can see that each man there has a possible weak point that a Soviet agent can exploit."

"I wonder why this was not picked up on initially," he said, looking over the notes. "You are right, of course. Taken as a whole they do not appear to pose a concern, but when you ferret out specific points as you did here, well..."

"That's how I see it too."

"The problem is, if we open another probe into these people, we run the risk of alerting any possible agent or collaborator, which would then drive them deeper. And there is also the problem of the work they are engaged in. You should know that these names you picked are part of about eight key people engaged in the research and development of the new systems."

"There is another way," I said.

"I am listening."

"Let me conduct the investigation with the help of some of my people on the force. We would be an unknown element and could use police methods and covers to move about."

"Hm. What you suggest has definite possibilities. What would you need from my side?"

"Access, mainly. You would have to give me full access to the labs and other research areas for a start. As you know, I have the clearance. I can arrange to set this up as a joint operation between our respective departments."

"And if you uncover...?" he started to ask.

"I can take action directly, after all, I am a policeman, officially. What happens after that will be up to you as head of security."

"So, if you do find any breach of security and you make an arrest, you will surrender that person, or persons, over to the intelligence service?"

"That's right. When it comes to the legal side of things, I believe the jurisdictional lines are pretty clear in cases involving national security and espionage, agree?"

"Yes, I do. It is good to be working with someone outside the military intelligence community that understands the distinctions."

"Well, the RCMP isn't exactly outside the military in Canada. For example, most of the military police; the provost corps, is made up of RCMP officers who transferred across."

"I forgot that point. So, how exactly are you going to proceed?"

"First, I will arrange for a surveillance teams to be put in place on the ones listed there."

"Carew, Wilcox and Stewart?"

"I understand Carew works here and at the facility at Shelburne?"

"That's right," Swanson said. "Key engineer on the electronics involved, especially because of his background in acoustics and such. Crucial areas in the Americans SOSUS operations. The work is divided between both bases. I assume you want to start as quickly as possible?"

"Yes," I said. "When I leave here, I will head to our HQ down on Hollis Street and start the wheels rolling. They will be touch with you to set up a liaison between our respective offices."

"Right. I see no more reason to keep you here. I will have all your clearances in place by the time you reach your HQ. All I can add is, good luck."

He reached a hand across the desk as he stood up which I accepted.

I left the base and made my way down to RCMP Headquarters. I found a parking spot down by the ferry terminal. I walked the short distance to the building entrance. Once I was inside, I reported to the duty desk, showing the constable behind the desk my ID, asking if a space had been set up for me. It was he said. He turned a sign-in logbook towards me and as I signed my name, he said, "Second floor; turn right at top of stairs; third door on the left. Can't miss it, sir."

I thanked him and headed for the stairs.

"Oh, one more thing," I said, stopping on the bottom step. "Is Inspector McKinnon in yet?"

"Yes sir."

"Thanks."

I rapped on McKinnon's door and opened it.

"Mornin'," I said as I stepped in. "Interrupting anything?"

"No," he said. "Just settling in for another day. By the way, Swanson called. Said you went to their personnel records files. Find anything?"

I must have given him a funny look because he said, "Jules and I keep in regular contact."

"Oh."

"Coffee?" he asked as I took a seat.

"Thanks. Black."

He reached for the phone and spoke to someone requesting two cups of coffee.

"He mentioned you picked out three names for a closer look."

"That's right." I pulled out my copy of the list I made from my inside jacket pocket and passed it to him.

He took it and unfolded it, spreading it on the desktop. He read it carefully for several moments.

"Interesting," he said, looking up at me. "Especially your reasons for singling them out. I get why you did and as I look at it now, I have to agree with your observations. Good work, by the way. I'm surprised Swanson or my people didn't pick up on it."

"I thought so too."

"Let me guess, you've convinced Swanson to let us investigate this matter?"

"Uh-huh. I'm thinking two-man teams for surveillance on Carew, Stewart and Wilcox for three days, maybe longer. I will conduct interviews with them as well."

"Won't that alert them and put them on their guard?"

"Possibly, however, I can just say it's part of a new security measure of doing spot checks. Besides my gut is telling me that Wilcox is the most likely to be our man."

He gave me a questioning look.

"He's the only one with a direct connection to the Russians from back in his university days."

"So why bother with the others?"

"I could be wrong," I said with a quick shrug. That brought a smile to his face.

"Okay. I'll set it up and get clearance from above. I assume you want me to handle this part here?"

"If that works for you, yeah. These are your people, after all."

"Happy to be working with you. I take it you plan on heading down to Shelburne?"

"Tomorrow. Been there?"

"Twice. Typical maritime town; fishing mostly. The navy is the biggest economic driver down there. You'll also run into a number of Americans; civilian technicians and scientists mostly, and some navy people."

"What exactly are they doing down there besides this SOSUS operation, that is?"

"The Navy and NRE are developing some sort of new landing equipment to be used on their ships that'll be carrying helicopters. Suppose to be able to land the whirly birds even in rough weather. The NRE has overall operational authority. They've been running everything from the start under the cover of the base doing oceanographic research."

"And the Americans are okay with that arrangement? I mean, it's been my experience whenever they're involved, they tend to run the show?"

"Not this time, in spite of the fact that Shelburne is a key station on their SOSUS system"

"So, who do I see when I get there?" I asked.

68

"Ask for Lieutenant Liam O'Carroll. He's RCN and heading up the security for the base. Decent sorta fella and willing to help. I'll call ahead. Oh, you need any help from the local detachment call me."

"Thanks, 'preciate it," I said.

We spent the next hour with him giving me a complete overview of the Shelburne base, its size, compliment of navy and civilian personnel and security measures. At the end of our meeting, I offered to take him to lunch which he accepted on condition that it was to be his treat, saying I was the visitor. I accepted.

Chapter Five

Josef Sokolov

Josef Sokolov sat in the large stuffed chair in their room at the Waverley Inn; a glass of Canadian Club rye whisky and ginger ale in his hand. He rested his head back with his eyes closed, listening to the music on the radio, thinking how he could get used to this lifestyle. Then he reverted back to matter at hand: their assignment.

It was not going to be easy in spite of the fact that the security around the navy base and dockyard appeared to be very lax considering the nature of the work being done...or so it seemed at first glance. While he and Ivanka were on their 'walk', he made it a point to watch everything around them, including being aware of anyone who might be paying attention to them. He saw nothing to raise any concerns which did not mean someone was not there. The KGB was very good at spying on their own and did it regularly.

His thoughts were suddenly interrupted by the sound of Ivanka entering the room from the bathroom.

"The pictures will be ready shortly," she said.

She had been in the bathroom working in the makeshift darkroom she set up. The KGB technicians had developed an ingenious system for quick film processing when in the field. When they returned from their dinner, she immediately went in the bathroom and set up the film processing equipment.

Fifteen minutes later, she went and retrieved the three by two and a half inch glossy prints; eight in all. He got up and joined her at the small table as she spread out the black and white prints; still damp from the developing tray. She held a magnifying glass out to him.

"There seems to be one or two points of interest;, here and here," she said, pointing at the pictures, specifically at parts of the ship's masts. "I don't know what these are, do you?"

"That one looks like it is possibly connected to the radar, I think. I don't know what that other one is."

"Something to do with this new system they have developed?"

"Possibly. I think I will show these to Wilcox. He should be able to tell us. I will make contact tomorrow." He turned away from the table and returned to the chair. Ivanka also left the table and took a seat on the only other chair.

"Do you feel up to talking about our other plans?" she asked.

"Of course, *meelaya*, always," he said warmly as he looked at her.

"Then we are agreed on our plan?"

"I see no reason to think otherwise."

"This could be the best chance we have to do this. If I see this rightly, we are almost completely out of their control here."

"True, but we must still step carefully, especially since you thought you spotted someone. I will begin to investigate our options as to who we can contact that will ensure our protection once we act. Why do you look so sad?"

"I was thinking that I would never see my home, my family, friends again. This will be bad for them...you know what the GRU will do when they find out."

"I know," he said. "But the danger is still the same if we go back, da?"

"Da," she said in almost a whisper. "Maybe if we are successful, we can..."

"It will make no difference. They are already wary of us so if we are successful and return to Russia, we could very well spend the rest of our lives in a gulag as a reward."

"Then why continue?"

"In case we decide to go somewhere else, another country. We would have something to trade for asylum."

"Oh."

She sat looking at him. He thought he saw a mixture of love and fear in her expression. He got up, setting his glass on the side table, and turned back to her, offering her his hand which she took.

"Come," he said, looking down at her.

When she stood up, he led the way to the bed.

* * *

Jesse Thompson

It was five-thirty when I finally returned to my room at Stadacona. The Orderly on duty, passed me a slip of paper with a note that Marie called a couple of hours ago. I was still full from the meal with McKinnon earlier, so I skipped on dinner, opting instead to have a cup of coffee and a piece of apple pie before returning to my room.

Back in the room, I went straight to the phone and dialed the base operator. Once she answered, I gave her the number to our Ottawa office and asked her to connect me. It was only four-thirty in Ottawa.

As always, I immediately felt a pleasant rush of happiness whenever I heard her voice.

"Deputy Superintendent Warton's line," she said in my ear.

"Hi doll, got your message," I said, sitting on the edge of the single bed. "What's up?"

"The boss needs to talk to you."

"Sounds ominous."

"I'll put you right through, hang on. I'll talk to you after he's done, so don't hang up."

"Gotcha."

"Jesse?" he said when we connected.

"Sir," I said.

"How's it going down there?"

"So far so good. I've found a few leads I'm looking into."

I gave him a detailed update on my progress and plans for tomorrow."

"Good work. McKinnon is a very able intelligence officer. Now to why this call. Our brethren in Washington sent a coded message on the DSTI secure teletype earlier today. By the way, is this a secure line?"

"Yes sir. I'm billeted in the officer's quarters at Stadacona and all calls are run through the secure communications system on the base."

"Good. Anyway, after the code boys deciphered the message, it seems that they were able to make an identification of the agent the KGB have sent. His name is Josef Sokolov; last known location here in Ottawa. Cover unknown, however, their records on him indicate that he always works with the same partner, a woman named Ivanka Chenko."

"That's it? Any idea if they are using alias'? Any descriptions?"

"No names, and the descriptions they have are pretty general and somewhat vague."

When he finished giving me what they provided, I noted that this Sokolov could be anybody, even me, for Chrissake.

"That's not very helpful," I commented.

"They said they were talking to other sources and maybe they will provide more information. Meantime, keep doing what you're doing and let us know of any progress."

"Yes sir. That it?"

"For the moment. Now go, oh, and try and not keep her on the line too long; I do have some work I need her to attend to."

Like I've said already...a sly old fox.

Once the line went dead, Marie was back on the line.

"I miss you," she said.

"Me too."

"You think you'll be there much longer?"

"Hard to say, baby. You know the job."

"Yes...yes I do. I gotta go, he's just beeped me. Take care. I love you."

"I love you too."

Then the line was dead and she was gone.

I decided to take a walk around the city, mostly to burn off some of the energy I was still feeling and to get a feel for the place. This was my first time here.

Halifax was an old city as evidenced by the age of many of the houses and buildings and some of the streets. Embedded rail tracks were still visible on a few of them from the days when a trolley system was used.

75

There were many shops, some with names I recognized from Ottawa and Toronto like T.C. Eaton's. However, the two most prominent impressions I got were from the military presence and the very active waterfront. The entertainment options were several taverns and movie houses; I counted at least five taverns and six of the other, although I heard mention of two or three others in other parts of the city.

As I walked around, people crowded the sidewalks; out shopping, since some of the businesses were open until nine. It felt good to be among the hustle and bustle of city folk again after spending so much time up north.

It was nearly eight o'clock when I arrived back at the base and my room. I turned on the radio, tuning into one of the local stations, CHNS, to listen to some music while I read the local paper before calling it a day.

Chapter Six

Jesse Thompson

The next morning, I arose early feeling refreshed. After a hearty breakfast, I went to the gymnasium on base for a brisk workout. Luckily, it had an indoor track so, I ran about five miles, then spent twenty minutes on the speed and heavy bags. By the time I left, I felt ready for anything.

I called McKinnon and was told the surveillance teams were set up and would be in place today. Forty-five minutes later, I was on the road to Shelburne.

I checked the road map I picked up from the RCMP depot when I signed out the car and traced my route, which was mostly on highway number three. The drive was about one-hundred-ninety to two hundred miles long. Roughly three, three and a half hours if I drove straight through. Which I opted to do, since I had a thermos of tea and a sandwich that I picked up from the mess hall.

The drive gave me time to go over what I knew so far and decide how to proceed. The trip was not absolutely necessary, but I needed to get a handle on what the work being done entailed and the level of security in place. Where were the files kept? Who had access to them? Could they be removed from the secure area, off the base even? How many civilians were employed on the base and how many actually worked on the projects? Were they locals or employed from away? There were just too many questions; too many chances someone could infiltrate or subvert someone on the base. Then there was Captain Jerome Carew.

I personally have no issues with anyone's sexual preferences until they become an issue, such as someone engaged on highly sensitive work which opens them up to exposure, or worse: like the present circumstance with Carew. But I was getting ahead of myself. I had no actual proof he was a homosexual. All I knew about the man to support my assumption was circumstantial, but I had dealt with this type of situation once before on a similar case. And, at the time, I had met with a psychologist specializing in the area of sexual behaviour and gained some insights and cues to watch for which would help me decide if Carew fit the profile.

That left the other two: Peter Wilcox and Kevin Stewart. Both worked on the projects in Halifax at Stadacona and the NRE: one on the CAST/1x sonar system and the other with the team developing the landing system for helicopters on ships in rough weather as well as the towed variable depth sonar array systems.

Of the two, I considered Stewart the most vulnerable to a KGB exploitation attempt through his son's health problem. There was nothing a father wouldn't do to protect his child. In this instance, that would mean securing treatment for his son which would very likely be expensive. In the past the Soviets had been known to throw a lot of money around if it furthered their cause.

Peter Wilcox, on the other hand, was not so easy a prospect. He seemed to be a solid, upright citizen. The only potential 'red flag' was his past involvement with a pro-Soviet organization as an undergrad at university, though he claimed it was only because of an interest he had in a certain young woman. I remembered there was no follow-up in his file about what happened to her when they did his background check. Did she stay active in the movement? Was she still a communist? Were they still in touch with each other?

I decided to call Inspector McKinnon later and ask him to take another look at the woman to see if she was still an active communist sympathizer and if there was a connection to Wilcox.

Jules Swanson gave me a fairly good, but general, overview of the work being done at the Shelburne base the day before, particularly in regards to the sonar systems and a new concept involving locating and tracking submerged vessels from the air using ship launched helicopters.

I had to admit, it was a novel approach, and I was beginning to see and appreciate why the Soviets would be interested. Since, if it worked, it would change the status quo in ASW, putting them at a distinct disadvantage.

I arrived in Shelburne late that afternoon and went directly to the base which was located at Sandy Point just outside of town. It was not much of a base, situated on the edge of Shelburne Harbour. The first thing I noticed was the absence of any security fencing or security check points. The only reason I could guess for the level of lax security was that the navy must be relying on the cover story of this place being an oceanographic research facility conducting studies for relevant government departments like Fisheries or Transportation and universities. The idea and principle were sound enough but... Most of the base was comprised of post-World War Two buildings with some obvious newer builds.

I rolled down a street looking for someone in uniform. Finally spotting a sailor wearing PO stripes, I tooted my horn and came to a stop. Rolling down the window, I asked if he knew where I could find Lieutenant O'Carroll. He pointed me in the right direction which was to the base administration building. I thanked him and drove on.

I found the building and parked in front. It was an unassuming building with no military personnel in view; for all intents and purposes it looked like any ordinary building you might see on any university campus; the only difference being the steel radio tower rising on top of the roof.

When I entered the main foyer, I was greeted by a middle-aged man in a business suit, sitting behind an information desk. The area was busy with a half dozen or so civilians; some in lab coats and carrying files.

"Yes sir, may I help you?" he asked when I stopped in front of him.

"I'm here to see Lieutenant O'Carroll," I said.

"Are you expected?"

"To be honest, I'm not entirely sure. My office was supposed to call but..."

"Let me check the logbook. Your name?"

"Thompson, Jesse."

I watched as he ran a long finger down the page.

"Ah, yes...here you are. He has been told of your visit, but it doesn't say when; odd. Usually there'd be a date and time. Well, no matter, you're here now, and you're in the book. The lieutenant's office is one floor up. Left at the top of the stairs then four doors down on the right. I'll ring and let him know you're on the way up.

"Thanks," I said, thinking it odd that he didn't ask for my ID.

Lieutenant Liam O'Carroll stood just inside the door to his office, looking down the hall as I rounded the corner at the top of the stairs.

He was a good-looking man: tall with a lean body, however, it was the red hair that caught the eye first, that and the bushy short well-trimmed beard and handlebar moustache.

"Inspector Thompson, I presume?" he said in a jovial voice.

I noted there was no hint of the typical Irish lilt you'd expect to hear from someone named O'Carroll.

"Welcome. Do come in," he said, offering his hand which I accepted.

"Hello," I said.

"To what do I owe a visit from the RCMP intelligence division?" he asked, letting go of my hand and returned to his chair. "DS McKinnon and I are in frequent contact. He called to say you were on the way down."

"I take it then, he also filled you in on my reason for coming here?" I answered, taking a seat in front of the desk.

"More or less, yes. Something to do with Captain Carew?"

"That's right."

"What is it you are hoping to find out that we haven't already learned from our internal checks?"

"A bit more than what was in the initial reports by your investigators, hopefully more background on his personal life."

"That sounds ominous. Can I ask why the sudden interest in that aspect of him?"

"I am not sure what you've been told, but the main reason I've been sent down here to Nova Scotia is because of a report received at DSTI from Washington alerting them of a possible KGB operation directed at the research projects being carried out in Halifax and here on the new ASW systems."

"I did receive a message to that effect a few days ago. But why the interest specifically in Carew?"

"In reviewing the personnel files of the key people on these projects, I was able to identify three people who could be open to possible subversion by or other links to the Soviets. Carew was one of them," I said.

"Interesting," he said, sitting back in his chair. "Care to elaborate?"

"At the moment, all I can say is there may be something that, if true, could make him vulnerable to a KGB approach. The problem being, what I have so far is purely circumstantial, so I want to step cautiously for the moment until I have something more substantial."

"I see. So, how exactly can I help?"

"Do you know Carew well? His activities outside of his work, close friends, bars he frequents...that sort of thing."

"Not really. I don't usually socialize with the scientists or other personnel, as a rule; after all, I have to maintain a certain detachment; arm's length as it were."

"So, you aren't aware of his activities then?"

"I didn't say that. We do monitor the key personnel as part of our SOP you know, standard operating procedure. Insofar as Carew is concerned, I believe he generally stays on the base in the barracks, although, he does make the odd trip off base, usually for an afternoon or a day trip; presumably taking in the area sights. Most of the staff does that."

"When he does go off base, is he usually alone?"

"Usually, yes."

"Do you happen to know if he has any social contacts down here?"

"You mean a woman? No, I don't, sorry. Come to think of it, I don't ever recall seeing him with a woman. Even here on the base, he doesn't seem to show any interest in the female staff; outside of the work, that is. Is that important?'

"Could be," I said.

"Oh...I see. You think he might be...?" he said, looking surprised.

"It's a possibility. If he is then he'd be vulnerable to exposure and blackmail by a foreign agent if they found out."

"I'll open an immediate investigation."

"I'd hold off on that for now."

"Oh?"

"I think if there is an incursion by the KGB, it'll likely be done in Halifax, since the bulk of the work is done there. Certainly, that's where most of the documentation is kept, as I understand it. Besides, I would think a foreign agent would stand out in a small place like this."

"Good point. Nonetheless, I will take steps to keep an eye on Carew. If I should uncover anything in that regard does the RCMP want to know?"

"Not necessarily, but I would definitely report it to Jules Swanson at Stadacona."

"Okay, thanks."

"By the way, when I arrived, I noticed there wasn't a perimeter fence or gatehouse, nor any guards. Unusual for a facility involved on work with such a high security rating?"

"It was decided that after the base was re-opened for its current use, it would be better if the locals thought of it has a research facility for oceanographic studies used by the universities in Halifax and the Oceanographic Institute. It appears to be working...so far. Security for the projects, as well as the American operation, is strictly and tightly controlled once you enter the facility."

"Even after dark?"

"This is a twenty-four hour facility; work goes on non-stop. And there are armed foot patrols within the buildings on the same schedule."

"And outside?"

"Of course; there is an unmarked car with navy shore patrolmen inside dressed in muftis. They make random drives around the general area. But, like I said, this is a small community where everybody pretty much knows everybody, so strangers would be noticed immediately, and word would be sent here within an hour or so."

"And that works?"

"As I said, so far, yes."

'Hmmm. Back to Carew. You say he billets here on the base when he's down here?"

"Yes, along with almost everyone else. It's part of their employment conditions."

"And when he's not here, does anyone else occupy his quarters?"

"Yes. This is a small base, so when we have visiting personnel, we double up; space is at a premium most of the time, however, it is usually kept empty. Most of the time the only ones in residence are the scientists and technicians. The non-military support staff is drawn from the civilian population who live in Shelburne or neighbouring areas. And that is still a pretty small group and easily managed."

"Well, I guess about covers it for me, thanks," I said.

"Seems like a long drive for something we could have done over the phone?" O'Carroll said.

"Maybe, but I wanted to get a better picture of what's going on here and, besides, I didn't want to discuss certain aspects of Captain Carew's personal life over the phone, no matter how secure, or where there might be a chance of anyone overhearing the conversation; it's still his personal life and reputation, after all."

"True. I have to say that's very considerate of you."

I nodded then stood up.

"One last thing. Given what we just discussed, could you keep an eye open for any irregularities or other activities and report them back to Inspector McKinnon?"

"No problem. I would be doing that anyway; keeping an eye on him, that is. I have no problem keeping McKinnon in the loop. Are you heading back to the city today?"

I glanced at my watch and saw it was getting on for five o'clock.

"Yes, it's still light enough and the drive should be quiet. If it's okay, I'll grab a quick bite at the mess before I go, maybe pick up a sandwich and a thermos of coffee?"

"Not a problem," he said, standing up. "In fact, if you wouldn't mind some company, I'll join you."

"Okay by me. How's the food, by the way?"

"Generally, pretty good, thanks to our American friends. Tonight's fare is beef, that means prime rib roast."

"Sounds good."

And it was very good. I had to take it easy though, since I had a long drive ahead of me and a too full belly would only make me sleepy.

I was back in my car and heading to the highway a half hour later and at Stadacona three hours after that.

The duty clerk stopped me when I entered the officer's quarters to let me know there were three calls for me. He handed me the telephone message chits with the names and numbers. I looked them over; one from Jules Swanson and two from Bryon McKinnon. I glanced at the wall mounted clock behind the clerk and noted the time: almost nine o'clock, too late to call either man, so I opted to call in the morning. Besides, I was beat from the round-trip drive and needed a shower. I signed in then headed for my room and a good night's sleep.

In the morning, after a run and hearty breakfast I called Inspector McKinnon first from my room.

"Bryon, Jesse," I said when he picked up. "You called?"

"Yeah," he said. "One of the surveillance teams on Carew reported in yesterday, saying they tailed him to an address up in the west end of the city. It's the residence of a prominent lawyer; a bachelor. He arrived at nine o'clock the previous night and stayed until almost one in the morning. I'm looking into this lawyer now. Given what we talked about concerning Carew's, um, possible preferences, I thought you ought to know."

"Appreciate it. If you can confirm the connection, it'll make dealing with him a lot easier."

"Shame really. I understand he's very good at his job. If this lawyer proves to be a homosexual, how do you want to handle it?"

"What Carew does privately is not my business; his potential exposure to blackmail by a foreign agent is. That said, as I told you, I'm here to identify and stop this KGB agent, if any, so anything you uncover I'll turn over to Swanson at naval intelligence with recommendation he work with you, if that's okay with you?'

"Not a problem for me. Jules and I have worked together before and got on okay."

"Great. I'm calling him next."

"By the way, how was your trip to Shelburne? Anything come of it?"

"I don't think I have ever seen a military facility doing such sensitive work run like that place. Christ, there wasn't even a fence."

"I know, but don't be fooled. The security there is very tight, particularly with the Americans involved and O'Carroll is one tough and competent intelligence officer."

"Yeah, I sorta got that impression. Well, at least the food was good."

He laughed at that, and we said our goodbyes.

My next call was to Jules Swanson.

"Lieutenant Commander Swanson's office," a sweet female voice said in my ear.

"Inspector Thompson returning his call from yesterday," I said.

"Oh yes, Inspector. I'm sorry, but the lieutenant commander isn't available at the moment; he's been called to a meeting at the Admiralty House."

"I see. I don't suppose you know when he'll be back or why he called?"

"No, sir. Sorry."

"That's alright. I'll call back later."

"Can he reach you before then if he comes back?"

"I'll be here at the officer's quarters for at least the next hour; after that I'm out."

"I will tell him."

"Thank you," I said, then hung up.

I spent the next twenty minutes going over what I knew so far, which was not that much of any real substance. I had a few things I wanted to look into, however, and I wanted to have a talk with Wilcox and Kevin Stewart.

I made a few calls and set up meetings with both men: one in half an hour with Stewart and one with Wilcox at three this afternoon.

Chapter Seven

Jesse Thompson

The Naval Research Establishment, the Canadian Navy's research facility, was set up in nineteen-fifty-two and located across the harbour in Dartmouth on Grove Street just under the bridge in an old red brick building with long rows of windows. It was at this facility that much of the developments on ASW and other maritime related technologies were worked on. It was where two of my suspects, Kevin Stewart and Peter Wilcox, worked.

I left for Dartmouth around nine-thirty and arrived at the NRE facility about fifteen minutes later. The building was a three-story red brick building with rows of high windows running along its faces. There was a chain link fence surrounding it with a manned gatehouse on the Windmill Road side. There were several other similar brick buildings inside the compound. I saw a number of metalwork frames lying around.

I turned into the security gate, taking my ID out and stopped. A uniformed navy rating came out of the guardhouse and approached my side of the car; I rolled down the window.

He wore the webbing commonly used by their shore patrolmen; except this time, he also carried a holstered sidearm.

"Yes sir?" the guard said, leaning down.

"Inspector Thompson, RCMP Intelligence," I said, passing him my identity card.

He took it and read it carefully, looking between the photo on it and me a couple of times before passing it back.

"What is your business here?"

"I'm here to conduct an interview with one of the civilian employees. Can you direct me to where I can find Kevin Stewart?"

"Stewart? Yes sir. You'll find him down in that building," he said, looking at and pointing to a small single story red brick building off to the right.

"Thanks," I said, putting my card back inside my jacket.

The guard stepped away from the car and raised the red and white striped barrier, waving me through. I eased out the clutch and rolled past him, nodding as I went by.

I found the area where Stewart worked and asked to speak with the supervisor or whoever was in charge of the section. A few minutes later, a man approached me, introducing himself as Mr. McLeod. I showed him my ID card and asked if he would arrange for me to meet with Stewart in a private room.

"May I inquire to what purpose RCMP Intelligence is here to speak with him? I thought all this business was done by the military?" he asked, looking concerned.

"Our section works closely with all security branches. This is a follow-up interview the RCMP has initiated of random personnel working on sensitive projects," I lied. "I shouldn't be more than twenty minutes."

"I was not informed of this. It is most irregular and damned inconvenient."

"Spot checks usually are," I said.

"Damn nuisance, if you ask me, but come this way. I will send Mr. Stewart along in a moment."

I followed him to a small side room with a desk and a couple chairs inside.

Five minutes later, Kevin Stewart knocked on the door and stepped inside.

He was wearing a white knee length lab coat with a slide rule sticking out of a breast pocket. He was tall, I reckoned around six-two or three, and slender. His hair was receding with signs of grey.

"Good morning," I said, standing up and offering him my hand. I hoped to put him at ease as I noted the worried look on his face.

"Harry, er, Mr. McLeod said you were with the RCMP Intelligence section. Is there a problem? Have I done something wrong?"

"No, not that I'm aware of," I said, indicating that he should take a seat. "I'm just doing a random spot check which we're doing at this and other facilities. Part of a new security procedure."

"Oh."

"How is your son doing, by the way?'

"My son? How do you know about that?"

I just looked at him.

"Oh," he said again. "Of course, he's doing the best he can so far."

"Glad to hear it."

"What does my son's medical condition have to do with security?"

"Let me answer that by asking you a question which should give you an idea why we're talking," I said. "Have you been in contact with anyone offering you the opportunity of treatment or other assistance for your child?"

"No... absolutely not. I see what you're thinking. I am a scientist and loyal to my country and I take exception to what you're implying."

I studied him carefully for a moment before speaking.

"You have to admit that your situation leaves you potentially exposed to a foreign agent's attempt to gain your cooperation."

"So, this is a witch hunt? You think I am a traitor?" he snapped, sounding genuinely angry.

"Not at all," I said, calmly, "however, as I just pointed out, you are vulnerable."

"If I was ever approached by a foreign agent, I would report him to the authorities."

Leaning forward, I studied his face. He was definitely upset and angry, but I could see no indications he was lying: no dilated pupils, no sweat. It took practice to control those emotions and physical reactions that betrayed the liars.

I decided to take a chance on him.

"Okay," I said, "I believe you would. That said, I will tell you we have received a report that the Soviets plan to send an agent, or agents, here to try and gather whatever information they can. If, as you say, you are loyal then I expect you to contact your superiors and Lieutenant Swanson, or our headquarters here, if anyone makes contact with you. Understand?'

"Yes," he said.

"Right. I think we're done here...for now. Thank you for your cooperation and good luck with your boy."

"Thank you," he said as he stood up.

I watched him as he left the room. I was about to get up myself when the door opened, and Mr. McLeod stepped inside.

"Is everything all right?" he asked. "I mean, with Kevin? He isn't in any trouble, is he?"

"Not with me," I said.

"Oh good. He's an important part of one of my teams working on a specific project. It would cause a significant delay if anything were to cause him to, uh, leave unexpectedly, as it were."

"You have nothing to worry about, at least not from us."

He gave me a funny look.

"His son."

95

"Oh yes, of course, there's that," he said.

"Well, thank you for allowing him time to talk with me. I'll get out from underfoot and leave you to your day."

We shook hands at the door, and I headed back to my car. Next stop: McKinnon at headquarters.

I found him in his office poring over numerous reports, seeing that made me appreciate how much I enjoyed being a field officer.

"'Mornin'," I said, stepping into the office. "Am I interrupting anything important?"

"Just my usual crap," he said, passing a hand over the mess of paper. "Come in and take a pew. I need a break anyway. Bloody administrative work. Days like this I miss the road."

"Highway patrol, was it?" I asked as I sat down.

"Yeah, until they gave me these." He pointed to the rank insignia. "What's up? Anything new?"

"I just came down from a meeting with Kevin Stewart over at the NRE."

"And?"

"I think we can knock him off the list."

"Reason?"

"Let's just say that he doesn't fit the mould to be turned, even with the promise of a benefit to help his son."

"I suppose you know best in these matters. Do you want to keep the surveillance on him?"

"Yeah," I said, nodding, "if only on the off chance he is contacted or approached, besides, I could be wrong, however unlikely that'd be. Anything come in from the other teams?"

He shuffled through a few sheets of paper then pulled one out.

"This is from the team on Wilcox; nothing suspicious or unusual. Same with Carew. Oh, by the by, this came in on the lawyer he visited; name, Walter Weinberg, age fifty-five. Never married, lives alone. He's a partner with one of the firms here in the city; specializes in real estate law. Member of several fraternal organizations; the Elks, Rotary Club and so on."

"Interesting," I said. "Seems to fit a particular profile among a certain community."

"I never thought of that before," McKinnon said. "But come to think on it, I think you might be right."

"Yeah, well, Like I said, Carew, or this Weinberg's private lives, are of no real concern to me, except for Carew. If he is a homosexual, then that exposes him to the potential for blackmail if a foreign agent were to learn of it. If it ever came to light, he'd lose his job, possibly be turned out from the military and, if it became publicly known, it would ruin his reputation."

"I'm surprised this wasn't caught by our friends up in naval intelligence, or our people, for that matter."

"It's been my experience that these people are very good at keeping that side of their lives carefully hidden away."

"You want to look further into Weinberg?" he asked.

"No, I don't think that's necessary. I doubt very much if Carew would be discussing his work with him or anyone else for that matter. What do you intend to do with this information?" I asked.

"File it until your job is done, then I have to turn it over to Swanson. He has to know about this since, as you pointed out, this makes Carew a high security risk."

"I agree. Right. Did you get that office set up for me that we discussed earlier?"

"I think so, why, you planning on working out of here for a while?"

"Off and on, if that's okay with you?"

"No problem. Hang on," he said, reaching for his phone. "Carol...check and see if that spare office has been set up for Inspector Thompson, please." There was a brief pause then he said, "Uh-huh. Thanks."

"There's a room two doors down on the left. Carol will show where. If you need anything while you're here use her. She's very good at her job," he said, hanging up the phone.

"Thanks."

I stood up and headed for the door.

His secretary's name was Carol Sutherland; a civilian. She was in her mid-thirties, attractive, well dressed and married.

"This way Inspector," she said as she stood and led the way.

"Jesse, please," I said, appreciating the view as I followed her, thinking of Marie back in Ottawa.

"Thank you and it's Carol. Will this do?" she said when we entered a small room with one window. It had a desk with a phone on it and a couple of wooden chairs.

"It'll do just fine," I said. "By the way, are the phone lines secure here in the building?"

"Yes. We have an arrangement with Maritime Telephone and Telegraph to operate on a dedicated service. Will you need anything else?"

"Not for the moment, Thanks."

"Then I'll leave you to your work. My extension number is two-two-nine if there is anything you need."

"Okay." Then she was gone.

I went and sat at the desk and reached for the phone. Time to check in with Ottawa.

"DS Warton's office," the love of my life said in my ear.

"Hi babe," I said.

"Well, hi yourself. I'm glad you called. I was about to call down there. Something's come in you need to know."

"Yeah. What's that?"

"I better let the boss tell you, just a sec while I transfer you."

The line went dead for a few seconds then Marcus Warton's voice sounded in my ear.

"Good. Glad you called," he said. "There's been a development. The Bureau has it on good authority that the Soviets have sent another agent to Halifax."

"Another one? They say why?" I asked.

"According to their source, it looks like the first pair they sent are under suspicion by the GRU and this new addition may have been sent to watchdog them; possibly to kill them, they don't know. You know as well as I do how the GRU operates, and ever since that embarrassment back in forty-six..."

"...they've tightened their internal controls over personnel working outside of Russia," I said, finishing his line of thought.

"Precisely, so be extra careful. They are hoping to get information on this new agent as well as photographs of Sokolov and Chenko. They'll send everything they get as soon as possible."

"This source must be very well placed," I remarked, "and is taking one hellava chance passing this information. It'd be bullet if they're ever found out."

"No doubt," Warton said. "What's new down there?"

"It looks like I've narrowed it down to two possibles."

I quickly filled him in on the results of my investigation so far, including bringing in McKinnon and his people to run surveillance on the possible people open to subversion by the agents.

"Sounds like this Wilcox fellow is the most likely candidate," he said when I finished.

"Maybe," I said, "but I still have to clear Carew before we take any action. I gave all the information to McKinnon. He's going to sit on it until this business is over, then he'll pass it along to Jules Swanson up at naval intelligence for any further action."

"It sounds like you have everything in hand, so I'll leave it with you. Check in again when you have anything new to report."

"Yes sir," I said, then the line went dead. I kept the phone to my ear because I knew Marie would be back on.

"How is everything going?" she asked when she came back on the line.

"Steady, but slow," I said. "Still no idea where the Soviet agents are; they haven't made any moves yet."

"I know what the boss told you, so you be careful, hear me?"

"You know me...the epitome of caution," I said, trying to soothe her concern.

"Never mind that, just be careful. I love you."

"Sorry. I love you too."

I hung up, thinking how much I missed her. Maybe it was time to take the next big step, after all, I knew with absolute certainty, I would never find a woman like Marie Chassion again.

It was time to prepare for my next call: Peter Wilcox.

He was an electrical engineer, specializing in radiography, or radar and sonar systems with emphasis on the properties and use of sound waves through water. According to his personnel file he was single, lived alone and, by all accounts, lived a normal life of a bachelor. His background check, indicated he was involved with a number of professional and fraternal organizations common with graduates looking to make the right contacts to help build their careers. His political affiliations did not raise any 'red' flags, except for a brief association with a pro-communist student group while an undergraduate. The investigators decided it was not an issue since his connection to them was an attractive woman with whom he had a brief affair. There was no follow-up on the relationship or the woman, as I had noted previously.

I picked up the phone and dialed Carol's extension.

"Yes?" Carol said, picking up after the first ring.

"Jesse," I said, "Can you see if we have anything on a woman named, Caroline Simpson. She's a lawyer and a known Communist sympathizer. She was a student at Dalhousie University and an active member in a pro-communist student group that Peter Wilcox was connected with when he was a student. Do you know if anything has come in yet?"

"Not that I have seen. The boss did ask me to look into it for him. Let me get on to our records department and get back to you."

"Okay, thanks. Oh, maybe you can call up to the campus administration office and see if they have any information."

"Good idea," she said. "I happen to know someone there. We went to school together."

"Great. If you get anything and I'm not here, can you send it to me at Stadacona?"

"Not a problem."

"Thanks again," I said, then hung up.

* * *

Pavlo Palyvoda

Pavlo Palyvoda sat at the wooden writing desk in the small bedroom he rented at a boarding house in the north end of the city. He carefully looked down the barrel of his handgun, which he had dismantled, checking for any hint of dirt. Satisfied, he laid it on the desktop beside the other components. The pistol was a Makarov 9mm; the standard handgun used by the Russian police, security service agents and the military.

Placing his hands on the desk he closed his eyes and took in a long slow breath, then he began to re-assemble the weapon. Twenty seconds later, he opened his eyes and looked at the gun in his hand. He picked up the nine round magazine and slowly inserted it into the gun's grip, snapping in with the palm of his hand then ratcheted a round into the barrel. He sat feeling the weight of the fully loaded weapon in his hand and, as always, felt the sensation of power slowly course up through his arm and flood his body. A hint of a smile, if it could be called that, creased his mouth as he recalled the number of men and women he had killed with this gun that almost felt like it was a part of him, a physical extension of his body.

For him, there was no greater aphrodisiac than the thrill of taking a life.

Eight years ago, he was languishing in a Siberian Gulag as a prisoner sentenced to life in prison for the brutal cold blooded murder of his wife and her lover, another woman. While there, he also murdered two more men who had tried to coerce him into a sexual relationship. It was then that he discovered his true nature: a natural born killer with no sense of remorse or morality.

That was when he came to the attention of the GRU who quickly realized his potential as an assassin.

They recruited him as part of a new section responsible for the assassination of political opponents and other perceived threats to their power. Since then, he had been credited with more than a dozen murders and proven himself a loyal and obedient servant.

Since arriving in Halifax, he set himself up with lodgings and made contact with his intended targets. All that he needed to do now was to await the order from Agapov to take them out. For now, his orders were to observe them only, reporting any suspicious activity or behaviour. Agapov told him he suspected them of planning to defect. If true, and they showed any signs of trying to make contact with Canadian authorities, he was to kill them then leave the city immediately. He was also told to take out anyone they were in contact with, no matter who that might be.

He took one last look at the pistol.

"Soon," he muttered, taking one last look at the pistol before returning it to the shoulder holster he wore. He stood up and grabbed the jacket draped over the wooden chair.

Chapter Eight

Josef Sokolov

Josef Sokolov was the first to wake up the following morning and, as always after a night of passion with Ivanka, he felt totally at peace. He slowly rolled his head on the pillow and looked at her sleeping face; a smile creased his face as he remembered.

After several minutes, he felt her stir as she slowly opened her eyes.

"*Dobraye Ootra,*" she said softly, looking at him.

"Good morning," he said. "It is."

He moved his head closer and kissed her on the lips.

"Come," he said as he lifted his head. "We have a busy day ahead."

"Da, but not immediately." Twenty minutes later, he rolled up to a sitting position on the edge of the bed.

Forty-five minutes later, they were sitting in the small dining room, enjoying a second cup of very good coffee.

"How are you progressing with sourcing out the local women's clubs that you mentioned before?" he asked, setting his cup down on the table.

"Good," she said. "In fact, I am invited to a coffee social this afternoon at the home of Mrs. John Goodman. Apparently, her husband is a senior executive at one of the companies supplying materials to the military and the shipyard."

"And you think there will be other women there who may have knowledge useful to us?"

"If it is the same here as in Ottawa, then yes. A number of these women are married to prominent and influential men, including in the military."

"We did acquire some very useful information as I recall. Have you discovered any other venues?"

"There is a Christian fraternal organization called the Knights of Columbus and a chapter of another such organization called the Elks. These westerners do seem overly fond of identifying with clubs. I suppose it must be some need to be seen as someone of importance."

"Ah yes, the hallmark of the class system," he said, nodding. "How did you manage to get an invitation, by the way?"

"I was at a women's dress shop, looking over the current styles. As it turned out, this shop, Mill's Brothers, is the only exclusive dress shop in the city, so it seemed a good place to try and meet well placed women."

He gave her a curious look.

"Women with husbands likely to be in important positions. How else could they shop there."

"Ah," he said, "good thinking."

"I struck up a conversation with a couple of women who were browsing the latest Spring fashions. I immediately got their attention when I let it be known that I was from Europe. I think being a foreigner must be some kind of qualification to enter their circle. Anyway, we got on well enough for them to invite me to meet some of their friends, hence a tea party."

"Very good and a very lucky meeting. What time is the meeting and where?"

"Three o'clock at her home. She lives down on the south end on Franklyn Street. What will you be doing?" she asked.

"I think it is time for another talk with Comrade Wilcox. I think I will make arrangements to meet him later this afternoon. In the meantime, I will return to the bridge and take another look at the ships. Let us meet back here for dinner and compare notes. Perhaps we could also begin thinking more carefully about how we will proceed when the time comes for us to leave."

"It will be difficult," Ivanka said. "We do not have contacts here, or know who to contact, or where to go."

"True," he said. "If necessary, we could turn ourselves into the police and ask for asylum."

"Really?" she said, looking incredulous.

"No, I do not think they could help. Maybe a local politician?"

"There must be a security service here; maybe the RCMP?"

"Yes, of course, you are right. While I am out, I will check out the local telephone book and look for a listing for the RCMP."

"Alright," she said.

They stood up and headed for the stairs and back to their room on the second floor. Once inside, he went to the phone, picked up the receiver and dialed.

"Wilcox," the voice said in his ear.

"It is me," Sokolov said.

"Oh good, I'm glad you returned my call." He was obviously speaking for the benefit of anyone listening. "I have that information you asked for."

"Very good. Three o'clock, my rooms."

"Yes, four-thirty would be better, okay. See you then." Then the line went dead.

He would be here at four-thirty.

* * *

Peter Wilcox

Peter Wilcox hung up the phone and casually looked around the office to see if anyone was paying him any attention. Everything seemed as per usual.

He went back to the spec sheet he was working on when Sokolov called, though now he was less attentive to the details on the sheet of paper. He always felt a bit on edge after talking to the Russian, thinking someone was watching him. His thoughts suddenly turned to the envelope in the drawer of his desk.

He got lucky when he was at the records room and managed to find several progress reports with technical data and formulae attached. He discovered later that the information did not have anything to do with the business he was working on, instead, it referred to another NRE project concerning landing helicopters on a ship at sea. Still, the information was important since it related to the navy's ongoing ASW research efforts.

However, there was another disturbing matter he needed to alert the Russian about. One that could have very serious consequences for him and Sokolov.

Four o'clock. The people in his office started to put their work away as they made ready to head home. Several said or waved good night as they left. Five minutes later, he was alone. He quickly opened the drawer of his desk and extracted the envelope he had placed there. He stood up and, after a quick look around, stuffed the envelope into his pants at the back, covering the exposed top half with his shirt. Ten minutes later he was in his car driving up to the security gate. The guard bent down and looked at him through the windscreen and waved him on; he waved back and eased the car onto the street.

He drove down Barrington Street towards the Waverley Inn and his meeting with Sokolov. Traffic was moderate, so the going was fairly quick. He turned up onto Harvey Street and parked in a vacant driveway half a block up, preferring to leave the vehicle out of sight of the hotel. He got out, locked the door and walked back to the hotel. He noticed the dark sedan as it drove slowly by heading up the street; the man driving it looking straight ahead, so he paid it no mind.

Once inside, he walked past the reception desk and ascended the wide, carpeted wooden staircase to the second floor. When he reached Sokolov's room he stopped, and after a quick glance back at the stairs, he rapped twice on the door.

A moment later it opened and Sokolov stood there at the side, gesturing him to come in with a wave of his arm.

"You do not look well, Comrade," he said as he closed the door. "Is everything alright?"

"Yeah...yeah," Wilcox said as went to one of the chairs and sat down. "It's just this business. I guess I'm just nervous, that's all. I'm not really cut out for this spy stuff."

"I understand. You said you have something for me?"

"I couldn't get any information on what you asked for, but I did manage to get a hold

111

of these." He stood up and retrieved the envelope from behind him, passing it to Sokolov.

"It looks like a test result report with some technical data. I think it has something to do with the navy's development program for a new landing apparatus for landing helicopters on their destroyer escorts. I believe it's part of their new approach to ASW; you know, using these helicopters to do sonar searches from the air. They've been working on this for some time."

Slokolov was scanning the documents as Wilcox spoke.

"This is very helpful," he said, looking up and dropping the envelope on the coffee table. "But what I really need is information on the new sonar systems used on their ships."

"I understand," Wilcox said, sounding a bit nervous. "But, like I told you, that area of research and work is way above my job classification and clearance level. The only way to possibly get what you want is to involve someone else and I don't really know anyone."

"But you have said that there are others sympathetic to our cause who also work in this area, yes?"

"Yes. From when I was at university, but I have not kept in touch with them, so I don't know how many are still active."

"Perhaps you can recall the ones who were, how you say, 'committed' and contact them on the pretext of catching up."

"Perhaps. Then what? Recruit them? I think that would be very risky, especially for me."

"No. You sound them out them leave the rest to me. If still loyal, then you will bring him, or her, to me, yes?"

"Okay, that'd be okay, thanks."

"Is there anything else I should know?"

"Funny you should ask," Wilcox said. "I overheard someone in the office talking on the phone, I think it was with someone over in the acoustics labs. Anyway, from what I could hear, it sounded like he had just been interviewed by someone in intelligence."

"Hmmm. Any idea why?" Sokolov asked.

"None. And I didn't ask."

"Curious. Keep your ears open for any more such bits of news and let me know. Well, if that is all for now, I think you should go. Be careful."

"I will." He stood up and left the room.

Shortly after Wilcox left, Sokolov decided to call Agapov and report even though he still had not much to pass on, except for this latest piece of information that Wilcox provided.

"You are late," Agapov snapped he answered the phone. "You were ordered to call in every day."

"There was nothing to report," Sokolov said, tersely.

"That does not matter. I need to know what you are doing, understand? You and Chenko are operating without any controls there."

"I would remind you; this is an open line."

"You dare to criticize me?"

"No; only to remind you." He knew that Agapov's line at the Embassy was secure and had a scrambler attached to it.

The line went quiet for several moments. Sokolov could envision Agapov fuming; he would have to be careful.

"Good point," Agapov said when he finally spoke again, although it sounded cold. "What have you to report?"

"Security here at their naval base is strange. I have not seen such peculiar procedures before."

"Explain."

"According to my contact here, security at the actual research facilities is tight and comprehensive, however, they have built a suspension bridge across the harbour which actually passes over their naval ships, giving a clear view of their external fixtures. This, by the way, also includes clear views into the shipbuilding facility and dry dock which is adjacent to the navy yard. We have taken pictures."

"So where does this leave you?"

"My contact has acquired some information; not what we are looking for, but interesting all the same. It has to do with the development of a new landing system for their helicopters on ships while at sea. According to him, it is part of their expansion of their ASW programme."

"Very good. How much longer do expect to take to complete your mission?"

"It is difficult to say, maybe another week, maybe longer."

"This should not pose a problem if, as you point out, the security there is so... loose. However, I insist that you call in daily regardless of there being nothing to report. Is that clear?"

"Da. It is clear," Sokolov said, suddenly sensing something was different this time. Did he suspect something? Or, was it because he and Chenko were operating completely on their own? Knowing Agapov as he did, he knew it was best to accept both propositions as being true if they were to make it to the end.

"Good," Agapov said then the line went dead.

Chapter Nine

Jesse Thompson

Peter Wilcox worked at the Anti-Submarine Warfare school and research laboratory located at Stadacona, so it would be a simple matter of going to his workplace for the interview. I wasn't convinced he would provide anything of real interest, since there were no 'red' flags in his personnel file, except maybe his brief connection with an on-campus pro-communist student group.

Sloppy work, I thought, at the very least, this group should have been marked for further investigation. It would be interesting to see what Carol was able to find out about this group and where the members were now. In particular the Simpson woman.

Then, as if she was reading my mind, my phone rang.

"Jesse, it's Carol," she said when I answered.

"What's up?" I asked.

"Something has come in on your request for information on those students who were part of that pro-communist group at Dalhousie. I think you might find some parts of it interesting in the context of your current investigation. I can bring it down. Oh, would you like a coffee since I'm coming down anyway?"

"Yes, please and thanks." I hung up, wondering why the information was so easily and quickly available.

A few minutes later, the door to my makeshift office opened and Carol stepped in; a mug in one hand and a file tucked under her arm.

"That was quick," I said as she set everything on the desk, giving me a questioning look. "Getting the information. I'm a bit surprised it was so readily available. Does that mean there is or was an open investigation on the group?"

I picked up the file, opened it and started to read the top sheet. It had a list of three names; Peter Wilcox was one of them. Below the list were several paragraphs outlining various activities the group was engaged in; mostly protests and the like.

"Apparently, the info was on file as part of the standard background checks we do for on civilians and companies with government contracts working on secret or higher classifications. It's standard operating procedure," she said as I read.

"I know that, but I wonder what prompted them to look at this group specifically?"

"I think you'll find three names in there who were members and have since been employed by the government and navy because of their respective specialties. Good luck."

"Thanks. By the way, who was the investigating officer and is he, or she, still here?"

"Everything is inside the file. But, as far as I know, the lead investigator has been posted somewhere out west. His name is Jack Fisher. I can try and locate him if you need to talk to him."

"That'd be great, Carol, thanks."

She turned and headed for the door. "Ring if you need anything else."

I opened the file and began reading.

It did not take long to discover that this group was a lot like so many other such groups springing up around the country, mostly on university and college campuses. As near as I could understand, the reasoning behind this activity seemed to share a similar point of view, namely, that the best way to avoid nuclear war was to accept communism which was epitomized in a popular slogan: Better red than dead.

For the most part, these movements seemed to be nothing more than an intellectual exercise with speeches and discussions in coffeehouses. So far as I knew, none of these people had posed any sort of risk to national security although, our section had opened files on a few of the more 'vocal' groups as a precaution.

I flipped a page and saw a short list of names; two men and five women with an annotation beside each one. Scanning down the list, I noted two that caught my eye: Charles Davis and Caroline Simpson. Both had an asterisk in ink, noting the fact that both were linked to Peter Wilcox.

Charles Davis had graduated with a degree in business administration while Caroline Simpson went on to law school. She passed the bar in nineteen-fifty-seven. Both were last reported as still residing here in Halifax.

I pulled the investigator's report on Wilcox again and quickly scanned the information. About halfway down the page I saw the name – Caroline Simpson. She was the woman the investigator stated having his eye on and was the reason he was there.

I reached for the phone.

"Yes, Jesse?" Carol said when she picked up.

"Can you find out any information on Caroline Simpson? Address. Where she works. You know, the usual background."

"I have already opened inquiries into her and Charles Davis."

"Bryon was right...you are good," I remarked.

"It's nothing special," she said. "It stood to reason you'd be wanting to know about these two. I'll bring you anything that comes in."

"Thanks," I said, then hung up.

Five minutes later, the phone rang.

"That was fast," I said, picking up the receiver.

"I'm good but not that good," she said with a chuckle. "No, Jules Swanson is on the line for you."

"Oh, okay, thanks." The line went quiet for a few seconds then Jules' voice said, "Jesse; Jules. Thought I would give you a quick call."

"Hi," I said. "Something come up?"

"I'm not sure, but I thought you would be interested in a bit of information that just came into my office. It seems that certain documents may have gone astray from the records room."

"Really? When did this happen?"

"In the last forty-eight hours, this according to Walter Small; he's in charge of the records department. They do random checks of filing to ensure any documents taken out are put back in their proper place as well as maintaining their visitor log. Anyway, once everyone checks out, the duty clerk goes around to make sure all documents were returned to their proper places and that's when she discovered one of the cabinet drawers was slightly open. Normally, this isn't a concern, except in this instance the file cabinet in question was in a section containing the most sensitive and highest level secret material and none of the three in the log book had clearance for that area," he said. "Small is running a thorough check of the files held in that particular cabinet."

"Okay, so why is this a concern for me?"

"Peter Wilcox," Swanson said."

"Yeah, so?" I said.

"According to Small, only three people signed in during that time frame: one was Peter Wilcox. If he was, in fact in that area, he was definitely over-stepping his clearance level and had no reason to be there. I only bring this to your attention because I know he is one of the people you have singled out for a closer look."

"Thanks, I appreciate this. Are you planning on taking any action from your side?"

"Only to the point of reviewing the security arrangements in the records section, particularly as they relate to access to that area. I have argued with my superiors that that section should have its own secure area. Maybe now they'll take notice. Anyway, that's not of interest to you or your investigation. I thought I would leave the matter of Wilcox to you as you requested."

"Thanks," I said. "In fact, I have been preparing to meet with him either today or tomorrow. This new information definitely changes how I'll approach him."

"I am not accusing him of any wrongdoing here, but I do not like coincidences," he said.

"Me either. I also think it's better to apologize later if we're wrong than miss nailing someone if he's guilty."

"Excellent policy. Oh, something else. I think he has an interest in one of my assistants; a young WAVE, Phyllis Ro,." he said, giving me her name and why he thought they might have been out together.

"Thanks. If it's okay with you, I'd like to come up and have a talk with her."

"Okay with me," he said. "When?"

"I'll just drop by, if that's alright. Oh yeah, best you say nothing to her or Small about my coming up."

"Okay."

"Let's meet up for lunch somewhere; my way of saying thanks. I'll leave the place up to you." Jules chuckled.

"You're on."

I hung up.

Well now, I thought, sitting back in the chair, this is an interesting development. I wonder what Wilcox would be doing in the records department?

I was fairly sure that he had a right to be there, as it would be the likely place where a lot of papers relating to his field of work were kept. It was interesting that, one: he did not have as high a security clearance as I would have thought and, two; that the most sensitive materials were also held there and not separated from the main body of materials. But that was Swanson's problem which he was aware of. Mine was to find the

122

most likely people a Soviet agent would be able to subvert to his task.

On that score, I decided it was time to consider checking the local hotels and inns to see if there was anyone matching the descriptions Marie sent me. This posed a minor problem. The RCMP did not have jurisdiction to run investigations within local communities, especially cities with their own police forces. I would have to run this by Bryon McKinnon before taking any steps.

I got up and headed for his office.

"Morning," I said when I stepped in and took a seat in front of the desk. "Got a minute?"

"Sure. What's up?" he asked as I settled on the seat.

"Back when Peter Wilcox applied for work with the NRE was he vetted by naval intelligence or us?"

"Both, as I recall, although most of the interviews were conducted by us. Why? Something turn up?"

"I just got a call from Jules Swanson to let me know there's been a breach up at the records department at Stadacona. Apparently, some documents seem to have gone missing. The man in charge, a Lieutenant Walter Small, reported it."

"Why does he think this is something you needed to know?"

"According to Small, three people had signed in during the time frame the documents went missing."

"Let me guess...Wilcox was one of them?" he said.

I nodded, saying, "I'm going make a surprise visit later to talk with the WAVE that was on duty. Also, he seems to think that the girl and Wilcox might have a social connection. By the way, I received a communique from Ottawa containing information on these agents that are here, just more background, but it got me wondering if a check on all the hotels and inns and such wouldn't be in order to see if they have registered."

"Good idea," he said. "Let me guess, you're thinking about the issue of jurisdiction, right?"

I nodded.

"Well, I think I can help you there. During the war, naval intelligence had a headquarters based here to oversee the security in the port and everything to do with the convoys. We also had an officer here as well seconded to them – Phil Mulroney; a sergeant at the time, but later promoted to Inspector. As you can image, it was a monumental task with limited manpower. However, they lucked out and ended up working with the local police department. By all accounts, it proved to be very successful arrangement. If my memory serves me correctly, there were two detectives, um,

John Robichaud and his partner, what was his name?...oh yeah, Pete Duncan. Mulroney worked with them on a half a dozen security cases dealing with enemy agents. Last I heard, Robichaud retired very soon after the war and moved back to Cape Breton, and Duncan took over as chief detective. He's still on the job, last I heard."

"Interesting," I said. "You're suggesting I bring this Duncan in on this?"

"Wouldn't hurt. He's a good man and a straight shooter. As far as I know, he still has a security clearance issued by naval intelligence. Besides, his people would be best for a job like this; they know the city and most of the operators."

"Okay, I'll talk to him."

"Good. Give me an hour to set it up. If he can offer assistance, he will be a big help, and we can coordinate between our respective forces."

"Thanks." I got up and headed back to my workroom.

McKinnon managed to set up the meeting with Detective Pete Duncan for two o'clock here at headquarters which suited me just fine, as I did not want to discuss my assignment in an open area, even if it was a police station.

Chapter Ten

Jesse Thompson

A couple of hours later, Carol showed Pete Duncan into my room.

He looked like a typical police detective: tall, dressed in a dark suit, trench coat and fedora. I noted that he also looked like he took care of himself, possibly working out on a regular basis. I liked that. He had a friendly face and a warm smile, although I sensed he could be serious and determined when needed. I liked that as well.

"Afternoon Detective," I said, standing up and offering my hand. "Thanks for coming down."

"Afternoon," he said, taking my hand. He had a firm grip. "No problem. Always happy to help out another cop."

"Take a seat. Coffee?"

"No, I'm good, thanks."

"Inspector McKinnon tells me that you've worked with us before, during the war."

"That's right. Me an' my former boss, John Robichaud. We were called in on a coupla cases naval intelligence was dealin' with at the time, mostly helpin' to find some

Nazi agents. We worked with an English officer name a' Michael Parks an' one of your people, Phil Mulroney."

"I know," I said. "A good man by all accounts."

"We thought so," he said. "So? What can the Halifax Police Department do for you this time?"

I briefly laid out the situation, including my role in the business.

"Bloody Russians," he said when I finished. "We had some bad experiences with them last time near the end. You say they are here again? What for?"

"We received a report from the FBI that the GRU; that's the Soviet opposite to the CIA in the States, is sending or has already sent KGB agents here to get as much information on the navy's anti-submarine warfare systems that is being developed here. My job is to stop that from happening."

"Meaning...what?"

"Meaning, if and when I find them, I will detain them and then turn them over to the local military intelligence agency for further action."

"So, what do you need from me?"

"A couple of things. We know the names of the agents and even have broad descriptions of them; it's a man and woman team, by the way. As you know, the RCMP has no direct authority to operate within your jurisdiction. Things like entering private residences, executing searches or

127

detaining citizens, which brings me to now and this meeting. I think your people have a broader knowledge of the city and the people living here. Both would be very helpful to my assignment."

"So, you want us to take up some of your legwork."

"More or less, yeah. We have some of our people on it already, but we don't have the manpower to do a thorough job. Specifically, to call on the area hotels and inns to see if the people I'm interested in have checked in somewhere. And to poke around the local shadier side of the city, if you catch my drift. We know these agents often will go to the local criminal element if necessary."

"Then what?" he asked.

"Then me and some men from intelligence will take them."

"Sounds simple enough," Duncan said.

"Yeah, but we both know it isn't always, right?" I remarked with a slight grin.

"Yeah. I know these people from past experience. They won't come easy. I have a bullet scar to prove it. So, if we find them, an' you go in to get them, you know there could be gunplay?"

"That's a possibility, yes, but we should be able to avoid that," I said. "The one thing about these people is they much prefer to stay in the shadows as much as possible."

"Well, I'm not so sure as you about that," Pete said, leaning forward a little. "I'm happy to give you any help I can, but I'm gonna hafta run this by my boss, who'll likely take it to the mayor for approval."

"I understand," I said. "How soon can you get the okay?"

"Probably within the hour. I assume you want us to start runnin' a check on the hotels as soon as possible?"

"Yes. Once you get the okay, I'll arrange to get you everything we have on the suspected agents."

"Right," he said, standing up. "I'll head back to the station an' get the ball rollin'. I'll call as soon as we get the word."

"Thanks Detective. I really appreciate this," I said standing up as well.

"No problem, an' it's Pete," he said with a smile as we shook hands.

"Jesse," I said.

I watched him as he left, thinking there went a good cop.

His call came at twenty to five. He told me that the mayor had given his go ahead and to provide full cooperation with our investigation. He also told me that he had already dispatched two of his men to begin the search. Now it was a waiting game. The bane of all police work.

I busied myself after he left with making preparations for my call on the records department at Stadacona and Phyllis Roy, the WAVE assistant. Peter Wilcox would have to wait until tomorrow.

The wall clock indicated that it was nearly three-thirty; time to head back to

Stadacona. I packed up and left, letting Carol know I was leaving. Fifteen minutes later, I was entering the records room.

Phyllis Roy was a pretty young woman in her early twenties but looked like she was fresh out of high school. She wore the black navy uniform: white shirt, black tie and skirt. I spotted her jacket on the of the chair she sat on. It had the red patch indicating she was in administration.

She looked up at me from her desk when I stopped at the counter.

"Yes? May I help you?" she asked, then, "Oh, I remember you. Inspector Thompson."

"That's right," I said.

"Lieutenant Small isn't here at the moment, I'm afraid."

"That's okay. It's you I want to have a chat with if you're not too busy to spare about ten minutes."

"Certainly," she said, sounding a bit wary.

"Relax. You're not in any trouble. This has to do with that report of some missing documents."

"Oh."

"Have you been able to identify which ones went missing yet?"

"It looks like several pages of drawing and specifications on the new landing apparatus for the helicopters."

"I see. Nothing on the work being done on the sonar systems?"

"Not that we can see," she said.

"I was told that three people had signed in during the time the documents could've gone missing, correct?"

"Yes, that's right," she said. "One was an officer off the ship being fitted out in the shipyard; one an engineer looking for field test reports and the other a technician from NRE looking for some spec sheets."

"Isn't the NRE over in Dartmouth?"

"Yes."

"I'd a thought that information would've been filed over there."

"Normally, yes, it is, but sometimes they send some of their files over here to be kept with related files from other sources."

"I see. How well do you know the people who come in here? I mean, there can't be that many, given the material held here."

"You're right," she said. "Mostly, they are people working on various sections of the projects. This place is sort of a central holding area for their respective documentation which, in a lot of cases, tend to overlap each other."

"Makes sense," I said. "I believe you know one of the people who signed in, Peter Wilcox?"

"We're friends, yes. Why?"

"It's part of a random spot check the RCMP is doing in the research and development facilities. His name is one of many I have been given to check up on. Does he come here often?"

"Not really. He usually calls when he needs something, and I look it up and give it to him by internal mail."

"On the time in question, why was he here?"

"He said he needed to see a certain set of data sheets."

"Couldn't he have asked you to get it for him as usual?"

I saw her cheeks redden slightly as she averted her eyes and said, "I think he came over to see me. We made a date."

"Lucky him," I said, which made her cheeks redden a bit more. "One last question. Was he and the others in sight of you at times when they were in here?"

She thought for a moment then said, "No, not always."

I thanked her for her help then left.

Chapter Eleven

Josef Sokolov

At the same time, elsewhere in the city, Josef Sokolov had decided to take advantage of the good weather and walk back to the Waverley Inn after his latest visit to the Angus L. MacDonald Bridge.

He was still amazed by the lack of overall security on the bridge, particularly the section that crossed over the naval ships berthed below. Most of the ships were leftovers from the war, some even older. Nonetheless, what was there constituted a significant force of surface ships.

He also noted one of the newer class ship being built sitting in the dry dock at the adjacent shipyard. It was a sleek destroyer type design with some interesting adaptations to it gunnery and electronics array visible in the rigging above the ship's bridge. There was also another one berthed at one of the docks with scaffolding around its rigging. He remembered Wilcox mentioning something about the new sonar systems being fitted to a ship for sea trials, perhaps this was it. If so, then what he saw had something to do with the new anti-submarine detection systems he was sent here to obtain. He was a little disappointed that Wilcox had as yet been able to get the information he wanted. If he continued to be unsuccessful he would have to consider other options to get the information: riskier options. He turned and started back to the Halifax side.

As he walked along Gottingen Street, he wondered just how far he wanted to pursue the mission in light of their plan to defect. After all, what would be the point of risking exposing themselves and possible capture; both possibilities would have a negative effect if they did manage to defect. Then, there was the potential danger posed by the possibility that Agapov had dispatched another agent to monitor them. Perhaps with orders to eliminate them if they deviated from the mission; typical GRU operational procedure.

It was just as he reached the corner at Cornwallis Street that he sensed something was out of place, like he was being watched.

He started to cross the street amid the crowd of people, still feeling uneasy. He continued on, relying on his training to see if he could identify the danger, if any. Using the reflections in the passing shop windows, he tried to pick out anyone who did not seem to belong. After another block and a half, he saw no one. He continued on, making sure to stay within the flow of pedestrians.

Pavlo Palyvoda

An ordinary looking man, dressed in workman's walked with the crowd. He was made frequent glances across the street, keeping his quarry in sight. He was thinking how easy it would be to kill Sokolov now. Just walk up behind him and shoot him in the back with his silenced pistol or skewer him with the stiletto knife he carried concealed up his sleeve. But not yet; not yet. He was ordered to follow him for now.

* * *

Jesse Thompson

I was finishing up for the day, putting all the files back in the folder when then phone rang.

"Yes?" I said after picking up the receiver.

"Sorry to bother you, Jesse, but there is a call for you from Ottawa," Carol said.

"Not a problem, I just finishing up."

"Hang on a sec while I transfer the call."

"Thanks."

A moment later I heard Marcus Warton's voice in my ear.

"Jesse?" he said.

"Sir," I answered.

"Good. I caught you. I understand Marie alerted you about another Soviet agent being sent down there. It has been confirmed. His name is Pavlo Palyvoda. According to the file the FBI have on him, he is part of the GRU's section they use for their 'dirty' work: physical intimidation, assassinations that sort of thing. The general view is, that based on past history, he probably is there to keep tabs on Sokolov and the woman. Makes sense since as far as military intelligence knows, the Soviets don't have any active operators working down there."

"Sounds like them," I said. "Makes one almost feel sorry for the bastards."

"Hmmm. I wouldn't lose any sleep over some of them disappearing some night."

"Did they also give any description on this Palyvoda?"

"Only a general one."

"So, how do you want me to proceed if he should become a factor?"

"First, with extreme caution. This man is believed to be responsible for at least five suspicious deaths. As to your investigation, use your own judgment. How are things standing at the moment?"

I gave him a detailed rundown on everything to date.

"Very good," he said when I finished. "Are you sure about bringing in the local police?"

"According to McKinnon, Detective Pete Duncan; he's head of their detective section, is a good and reliable cop. He and his former boss, Detective John Robichaud, were actively involved with naval intelligence during the war and both were cleared and given security clearances. Plus, Duncan has experience with the Russians; apparently they had a few run-ins with them back in forty-five, one resulting in his being shot."

"Okay, I'll trust to your judgment. If there's nothing else?"

"That's it for now. I'll check in again after I interview Peter Wilcox tomorrow."

"Okay, oh, Marie has left for the day, but I'm sure she sends her best."

"Thanks."

Then the line went dead. I held the phone for moment then, once connected to an outside line, I dialed.

"Detective section," a male voice said after two rings.

"Hello," I said. "Is Detective Duncan still there?"

"Yes. Who's callin'?"

"Inspector Thompson. RCMP."

"Oh right, jus' a sec, I'll transfer ya."

A moment later, "Duncan."

"Hi Pete, it's Jesse."

"What's up?'

"I just got off the phone with Ottawa. Looks like our friends have sent another agent to Halifax. His name is Pavlo Palyvoda." I gave him the description Warton passed on. "He is a known assassin with the GRU, their intelligence arm. The view he is here to watchdog the other two, but he could also be here to kill them."

"Jesus what sort of people are these people?" he said.

"I know. I'm letting you know because once your people start poking around there's a good chance the Soviets will get wind of it. I don't think there any danger to your men from Sokolov and the woman but..."

"But possibly from this Palyvoda asshole, right?"

"Right."

"So, what're tryin' to tell me?"

"To be careful. If your men come across this man, tell them to back away and report back to you or us. Specifically, Inspector McKinnon at RCMP Headquarters; he's in on this business. We'll then let the military police deal with him."

"What if he opens up on my men? Or kills a civilian?"

"Then he's all yours." I said. "My interest is with the other two and anyone working with, or for, them. Although, if that comes to pass and you do take him, it might be far less headaches for you if you turn him over to the military. If, as you say, you've dealt with these people before then you know what I'm talking about."

"Diplomatic bullshit."

"You got it. I know this rubs the wrong way, but that's the reality these days."

"Yeah, I get it, but I still don't like it. Okay. That it?"

"Yeah, for now."

"Thanks for the heads-up. Talk again later." Then the line went dead.

I sat looking at the phone for a moment after hanging up, thinking about why Duncan sounded so peeved. As a cop, I understood his feelings about some government loophole that lets killers and criminals walk away from their crimes. But since Hiroshima and Nagasaki and the emergence of Communism in Russia everything had changed. It was a new and more dangerous world now, requiring new rules. I was thinking McKinnon was right about Duncan.

I checked my watch and saw it was getting late, so I got up and, taking the file, headed for Carol's office. She was also closing up for the day when I arrived.

"Good," I said. "Caught you in time to return these papers."

I handed them over to her and she took them, putting them into a drawer of a steel filing cabinet behind her desk. Once safely inside, she closed the drawer and locked it.

"Thanks. Can I offer you a ride home?" I asked.

"No thanks," she said with a smile, "Bill, my husband, always picks me up."

"Well, at least let me walk you out."

"Okay. I'd like that, thank you."

We left the office which she also locked and headed for the stairs. We chatted casually as we made our way to the street. I saw an older looking car parked by the curb on Hollis Street with a man sitting behind the wheel smoking a pipe. She waved at him then turned to me. "Good night, Jesse. See you tomorrow."

I watched for a moment as she walked to the car and stepping around the rear got in on the passenger side. I suddenly thought of Marie with warm feeling inside.

As I drove back to Stadacona, I started to work out a plan for tomorrow.

Chapter Twelve

Palov Playvoda

Pavlo Palyvoda had been up at a local bootlegger's house for a drink and was talking with a few men who were there playing cards. He liked being around working men and prostitutes; it was his element, where he felt 'at home'. He saw that one man in particular, was watching him, trying to appear nonchalant about it, then ten minutes later he was gone.

Pavlov finished his drink and, not seeing anything particularly interesting in either of the two middle aged women in the room, he paid up and left. Once outside, he started back to his room at the boarding house. He had the feeling that he was being watched, but could not detect anyone.

His instincts were on full alert as he walked down Duffus Street under the deep shadows of the trees. It did not matter that it was already very dark since it was almost midnight. He remembered one of his instructors back in Russia drilling into the heads of the recruits, 'there can never be too much shadow'. It was one of the best ways to stay alive and free of capture.

Turning at the corner of Lynch Street, he quickened his pace briefly then slowed long enough for a quick glance over his shoulder. A second or two later, he saw the car slowly turn the corner. Continuing on, he headed for the house about seven buildings farther along and went up the three steps to the door.

The house was owned by a sixty-year-old widow woman with no children. She showed no interest or suspicions about him when he approached her to let the room. All she seemed to care about was that he could pay the rent. He had 'cased' the house when he took the room, so he knew where the back door was located. His room was at the back of the house beside the kitchen. He unlocked the door and went in quietly, making his way to his room.

The air inside still smelled slightly of the fish dinner the landlady had cooked earlier and of the pungent stink of the Russian cigarettes that he smoked; what people called firecrackers. As he neared the door he saw light emanating from under the door. A moment later, he saw a shadow move through the light; someone was in his room. It could only be the old woman. But why, he wondered. Then the light went out and he heard her stepping to the door. He quickly moved to stand back to the wall beside the door, drawing his knife.

The door opened outward, so he was behind it when she stepped through, looking furtively into the semi-dark kitchen. She did not hear him move as he stepped up behind her and clasped a hand over her mouth while he drew the cutting edge of the blade across the left side of her neck, slicing neatly through the jugular artery.

He held her tightly as her life blood flowed down her chest, staining her night gown. Moments later, he felt her body begin to sag as her life slowly left her. He eased her body to the floor, laying it beside the oil burning stove. Looking down at her face, he saw her eyes and the confusion in them and her mouth moving in a last attempt to say something. He turned way abruptly.

He cleaned the blade on a hand towel hanging from the oven door then went into his room. Time to go, he thought as he retrieved his travel bag and started to pack the few belongings he had with him. Five minutes later and satisfied there was not any trace of his having been there, he left the room. Stepping over the now dead woman, he went into the front room where the telephone was located. Picking up the receiver, he dialed the number Sergi Agapov gave him before leaving Ottawa.

"Yes, hello," a woman said, her voice thick from sleep.

"This is Comrade Simpson?" he asked.

"Y...yes, who is this?'

"My name does not matter. I am instructed to contact you if I need assistance."

"I understand," she said, now suddenly very much awake. "What do you need?"

"A safe place," Palyvoda said bluntly.

"Where are you now?"

He told her the address.

"Good. You are close. How well do you know the city?"

"Not well," he answered.

"Okay. I know where you are. I will be there in thirty minutes. Are you able to stay put until I get there?"

"Da."

"Okay. In thirty minutes, maybe sooner," she said, then the line went dead.

He hung up and headed for the back door and stepped outside, heading for the alley and the street at the end.

* * *

Jesse Thompson

I felt that I would soon be able to lay hands on the two Russians if Duncan's men were successful. However, I realized that, like him, I was hamstrung as to what I could do beyond running them out of the city. Unless of course, I could catch them with secret documents or other materials. I knew this would only delay the Soviets before another incursion was attempted. I knew the only way to shut any breach down was to nail their collaborators: the source of the leaks.

It was during my dinner in the wardroom that I put together a plan of attack.

I would deal with Sokolov and Chenko myself and, as for any conspirators I uncovered along the way, I would secure enough evidence to nail them and I would then turn that over to Jules Swanson and Bryon McKinnon for further action. In that regard, I decided to scale back my list from three to two; Kevin Stewart, I decided, was the least likely target for the Soviet agents. That left Carew and Wilcox.

The next morning, I headed down to RCMP Headquarters to catch up on any overnight developments and put together my day. I had made up my mind to talk with Captain Jerome Carew first, mostly because the only suspicious thing about him so far was a possible 'liaison' with a single lawyer who might be a homosexual. If true, then I would strike him from my list and let Jules Swanson deal with him.

Carol had beat me in by half an hour. She gave me a warm smile when I leaned in and said good morning. There were no messages or other information for me, although she said she had asked her friend, up at the Registrar's office at Dalhousie, to look up the information I requested earlier. She would call her later and see if there anything yet.

I stopped at the coffee urn and poured a mug then went to my work room.

After I finished the coffee and reviewed my notes, I reached for the phone and dialed the number for the laboratory where Carew worked.

"Good morning, sonar lab," a young sounding female voice said in my ear after two rings.

"Good morning," I said. "Captain Carew, please. Inspector Thompson, RCMP calling."

"Captain Carew is not in today. Can I take a message?"

"Oh. I was under the impression he would be there today."

"He was supposed to be, but he was called away late yesterday to the Shelburne facility. As far as I know, he left late yesterday afternoon."

"Do you know when he will be back?"

"Maybe later today, or early tomorrow."

"Does he get called away a lot?" I asked.

"Often, yes., usually it's just for a day, maybe two. Do you want to leave a message?"

"No, that's okay," I said, "I'll call back. Thanks." I hung up. Well, I thought, that leaves only Wilcox.

"I was packing up my files and notes when the phone rang. It was Carol.

"I have Detective Duncan on the line," she said.

"Thanks, put him through," I said.

"Jesse?" Pete Duncan said.

"Yeah, what's up?"

"I think we might've hit pay dirt. One of my men was talkin' with one of his snitches up at a bootlegger's place in the north end, on Duffus Street, I think. Anyway, it's one of several places we've been keepin' an eye on for runnin' illegal poker games, bootleggin' and hookers. It seems there's a foreigner bin seen in the neighbourhood. The snitch apparently followed him after he left to a roomin' house on Lynch Street. It's the first right up from Barrington off Duffus."

"Jesus that was quick work," I said.

"Small city. How do you want to handle it?"

"I'll check it out myself first. If it's just one person it might be Palyvoda. I don't want to spook him into doing something rash. Did this guy say if he fit the description, I gave you?"

"No. He didn't get a look at him an' that description you gave me was pretty broad you hafta admit. I mean, it could fit just about anyone."

"Yeah, I know," I said. "Couldn't be helped. It was all I had. Give me the address where this man is staying and directions."

Pete gave me everything I needed which I wrote down in my notepad.

"You thinkin' of goin' up there on your own?" he asked.

"No. I thought I'd take one of our constables with me, why? That a problem?"

"Not for me, but if somethin' happens..."

"I get your point," I said. "Okay, what do you suggest?"

"Maybe I best come along with you, you know, jus' in case."

"Happy to have you along."

"When do you want to head out?"

"I can pick you up in twenty minutes, if that works."

"Yeah, okay. I'll be outside waitin'."

He gave me directions to the parking area at the side of the new station just below the corner of Brunswick and Duke streets. It was hard to miss. The station, formerly located in the old city hall building had recently moved into the old city market building; a large stone building that took up a significant stretch of Brunswick Street. The most striking aspect of its architecture were the three rows of windows that circled the structure.

"See you then." I hung up the phone.

I made a quick call to Jules Swanson at Stadacona to give him an update, turning down his offer to send someone with me at the end of the call, saying it might be nothing, and that one of the city detectives was already there. Then I popped in and let Bryon know, telling him I would radio in once I figured out what the situation was at the boarding house.

Just as I was about to take off, Carol stopped me to say her friend up at Dalhousie was able to get the information I requested.

148

I asked her to get it, and I would check it out when I got back.

Once back in my car, I headed my rendezvous with Pete. I drove down Lower Water Street to Duke Street, turning up the steep street. Pete was standing on the sidewalk. I tooted the horn as I turned onto the side street at the rear of the building. He crossed over and got in on the passenger side.

When we arrived on Lynch Street, he pointed to a point halfway down on the left side. It was a typical residential street: concrete sidewalks on both sides; tree lined with streetlamps situated at evenly spaced locations. The houses were all wooden structures and followed similar designs: two story on brick foundations. All having been built after the Halifax explosion back in nineteen-seventeen. Overall, it looked like a nice place to live and raise a family.

"I think that's the house," he said.

I slowed and eased the car to the curb.

"How do you want to handle this?" I asked, deferring to him.

"Most of these places have alleyways leading to the backyard an' a rear door," he said in a matter-of-fact tone of voice. "Normally, one of us would cover the back while the other went to the front. But this isn't exactly a normal situation."

"I think from a purely legal standpoint it'd be best if you took the front. You're the

149

one with the legal authority here. I can watch the rear."

"Good point."

"Just be careful," I said. "Remember, this guy isn't one of your local hoodlums; he's likely to take the hard way."

"Gunplay?"

"It's possible," I said, "so, go ready."

He nodded, indicating he understood me.

"Give me a few moments to get into position...that the alley?" I asked pointing at the space between two houses before getting out of the car.

"Yeah," Pete said as I reached for the door handle. "Good luck."

"Thanks. You, too."

I got out and crossed over to the opposite side of the street, making my way to the alleyway. As I neared the entrance, I heard Pete get out of the car. I took a quick glance and saw he him cross over towards the front of the house. He held his service revolver in his hand down by his leg. I moved into the alley which was about four feet wide. When I reached the end, I pulled my gun and waited.

Five minutes later, Pete stepped out backdoor and waved me over.

"You better take a look at this," he said. I noticed he had re-holstered his weapon. I did the same.

"Whaddya got?" I asked, stepping into the kitchen behind him.

"See for yourself." He stepped aside so I could get a clear look into the room.

There, crumpled on the floor beside the cast iron oil stove in a pool of blood, lay the body of an elderly woman. Her neck had been neatly cut on the left side completely severing the jugular artery.

"Jesus Christ," I said, looking away from the sight.

"How long do ya reckon she's been dead?" Pete asked.

I bent down and lifted one of her arms.

"Rigor hasn't set in yet, so maybe a couple of hours," I said, gently laying the arm back down and standing up.

"Yeah, be my guess too," he said. "I gotta call this in an' get the wagon up here."

"Okay. If you're alright with this, I'll see if he's left anything behind."

"Yeah, go ahead."

I headed out of the kitchen and began a quick search of the house while Pete went to find a phone, quickly finding what had to be the lodger's room. I went in and did a thorough search, turning up nothing; not that I expected to. The Soviets trained their agents well; excellent killing and cleaning skills, among others. When I finished, I joined Pete in the small front sitting room.

"Anythin'?" he asked when I stepped inside.

"No," I answered. You?"

"Not much. Her name was Shirley Jacobs. Looks like she was a widow; her husband killed in the war; a merchant seaman. I'm guessin' his ship was torpedoed. Don't see any photographs of kids."

I could see he was doing his best to keep his anger under control.

"My men are on the way an' the ambulance should be here in a few minutes. So, if you want to head out, I got this. There's not a lot you can do here anyway."

"Yeah, okay," I said.

"This won't take long once my men show up."

"Thanks, Pete. Tell you what, let's meet up at my office down at RCMP headquarters, around four."

"Yeah, okay. I know the place." He nodded then turned and headed for the motel's office. I made my way back to headquarters. I called Jules Swanson first and filled him in then I stopped at Bryon McKinnon office and filled him in.

"I just heard," he said, when I finished. "I'd say that sorta confirms the reports you've been getting."

"Looks that way," I said. "Quite a way to announce your presence."

"How's he doing? The cop?"

"Pete Duncan. He's pissed off. I arranged for Duncan to come down to headquarters at four o'clock. He's more or less taking over the show; it happened in his jurisdiction."

"Gotcha. Think he'd mind if I sat in?" Bryon asked.

"Don't see why he should, after all, it looks like it's shaping up to be a joint operation and this is your patch."

I stopped at Carol's desk when I left his office to let her know I was back and to alert her to Pete's arrival.

"That poor woman," she said. "It must've been awful to see something like that."

I could not think of anything to say, so I just stood there. She was obviously upset and just a bit angry.

"Things like this don't usually happen here, you know, I mean killer agents running around," she said with what I thought was a hint of accusation in her tone of voice.

"Times have changed," I said. As if that explained everything. It didn't, of course.

"I'm sorry, Jesse, I didn't mean to..."

"Not a problem," I said, cutting her off. "I didn't take any offence."

"Thank you." She straightened up slightly and took on her usual demeanour. "I'll bring the files down to your office along with the information on those two former students you requested. Coffee?"

"Yes, to both, thanks." I turned away and headed for my work area.

I was sitting at my desk at headquarters looking over the information on Charles Davis and Caroline Simpson Carol had obtained and left for me. I needed something to occupy my mind and to help get rid of the image of the woman lying on her kitchen floor in a pool of blood.

Both persons of interest were students at Dalhousie at the same time as Peter Wilcox and were members of a pro-Soviet activist group that existed on campus at the time. Groups like this one were becoming common on many campuses throughout North America back then, arising out of fears created by the advent of the atomic age among other things. Stalin and the Soviets had become a major de-stabilizing force since the end of the second world war with the effect of creating a time of high anxiety and fear of another more devastating war. These groups and similar movements gave rise to such popular phrases as, Better Red Than Dead and the Red Scare. It also produced notable political extremist movements as the House Un-American Activities Committee led by Senator Joseph McCarthy in the United States.

According to the records Carol obtained from the Registrar's office up at Dalhousie, Charles Davis graduated with a BA Degree in Business Administration, and was last reported to have gone on to receive a certification from the Nova Scotia Teacher's College and was teaching at a school in Truro. He was married and had two children.

As for Caroline Simpson, she received her Law degree and was practising here in the city from her own office as a public defender. According to a note appended by a follow up interview, she was still an active supporter of the communist movement. Interesting, I thought.

I reached for the phone.

"Carol, Jesse," I said when she picked up.

"Yes?" she said.

"I've been going over the information you got from your friend at Dalhousie. I see that Simpson is working as a public defender, but it doesn't say for which law firm. Also, can you check and see if there is any record of an active communist party or group here in the city?"

"As to your first question, she's working out of her own office with two other lawyers, both women, and I can say with certainty that the communist party has no visible presence here, not formally at any rate."

"And you know this...?" I asked.

"We ran an investigation a couple of years back for headquarters in Ottawa as part of a national program undertaken by the Department of National Defence on pro-Soviet groups and their activities."

"Ah, thanks. Can you dig up an address for Simpson's office for me?"

"Sure thing. I'll get it you right away."

"Thanks again." I said, then hung up.

Pete Duncan arrived at ten to four. Carol led him down to where I was working. He did not look happy.

"Thanks," I said as she turned to leave. "Oh, yeah, let Bryon know he's here will you."

155

"Already did. He'll here in a few minutes."

I smiled as she left, closing the door behind her.

Pete gave me a questioning look.

"Inspector Bryon McKinnon," I said. "He's the lead investigator for the area and asked if he could sit in. I said it was okay since you two will likely be working together on this matter from here on. Besides, I was led to understand you two knew each other?"

"Uh-huh. We met a year or so back. This mean you're not handlin' this?" he asked as he sat down.

"Pretty much, yea," I said. "My primary business are the Soviet agents that are here and identifying who they are working with. This business with the dead woman is your problem. The RCMP's interest extends only so far as the killer was possibly a Soviet agent, then it becomes a joint jurisdiction issue. However, since it might involve national security, he has the authority to intervene and assist local police."

"Yeah, I know how the game works. Learned all about it back in the forties. I don't have a problem myself. I like workin' with your people."

"Good," I said. "So, anything new?"

"One of my men out checkin' the hotels thinks he may have come onto somethin'. He was down at the Waverley Inn on Barrington Street. It's close to the rail station. Anyway, accordin' to the registration clerk, five foreigners have registered in the last four days; two couples and one man. I think we can rule out the single fella if you're information is correct an' we're lookin' for a couple."

"I agree," I said.

He pulled out a sheet of paper and passed it to me.

"Here're their names."

Just at that moment the door opened, and Bryon McKinnon stepped in. He closed the door and pulled a chair over and sat down.

"Good to see you again, Detective," he said, looking at Duncan and extending his hand.

"Yeah, you too," Pete said, accepting the offered hand.

"Bad business this killing. Have you learned anything more than what we know already?"

"Not much. All we've managed to get so far is that she usually rented out a coupla spare rooms to travellers passing through, or here on business. She manages on a widow's pension which isn't much, so she needed the extra money. Accordin' to some of her neighbours, she was somethin' of a 'nosey parker'; regularly poked into other people's business. If her killer was this Soviet agent Jesse told me about, an' he caught her snoopin' around...?

"Possible," Byron said. "Definitely possible. And you found nothing at the house that'd help figure out where he might've gone?"

"Clean as a whistle," Pete said.

"What about you?" he asked, looking at me. "Anything?"

"Not really," I said. "Although Pete was just telling me that one of his men, checking the area hotels, has discovered five foreigners who registered at the Waverley Inn in the last four days." I passed him the list of names Pete gave me. "And Carol was able to get her hands on information for two fellow students that were at Dalhousie the same time as Peter Wilcox."

Pete gave me another questioning look.

"Another line of inquiry to do with my investigation but may be a link to this case."

"Let me guess," Bryon said, "part of that pro-Soviet student group?"

"Uh-huh," I said, nodding. "She also found out the woman Wilcox claims was his reason for joining the group seems to be operating here as a public defender working out of her own law office. Carol's getting me her address as we speak."

"And you think this, what was his name, oh yeah, Palyvoda, might possibly know her and try to make contact?'

"It's a thought," I said.

"Thin. Really thin."

"Most of what we do usually is."

"I take it you're talkin' about the possible killer?" Pete asked.

"Yes," I said.

"If he does contact this lawyer, what then?"

"If he has, I'll turn the matter over to you to handle. Like I said, my only concern is shutting down any security leaks and that makes her mine for the moment."

That seemed to satisfy Pete who sat back and nodded.

Chapter Thirteen

'And now for the latest news. Early this morning, the body of an

elderly woman was discovered in her home on Lynch Street in

the city's north end. According to sources, she was the victim of

a brutal attack. The police were on scene but refused to offer any

comment except to say they were treating the incident as a

possible break-in resulting in a homicide.'

Josef Sokolov

Josef Sokolov entered from the bathroom. Ivanka Chenko stood over the portable hot plate they purchased idly moving the eggs around in the pan as she listened to the news report on the radio. Poor woman, she thought, just as

"What was that?" he asked, looking at the radio.

He was wearing shoes and pants with a sleeveless undershirt tucked in at the waist; a towel was draped over his shoulder as he patted his face dry with one end. He went to her and kissed her on the cheek.

"Some poor old woman was killed last night," Ivanka said, lifting the pan off the stovetop and sliding the eggs onto a plate.

"Bad things happen," he said as he sat at the small wooden table.

"I know, but it is unusual for such things here." She placed the plate in front of him and turned back to reach for the pot of coffee she made earlier.

"Meaning?"

"The information we have on this city did not suggest that this type of criminal activity was common."

He gave her a questioning look.

"This incident stands out because of it does not fit the background information that was compiled on many of Canada's cities, especially ones with seaports. Crime here in this country seems to be primarily economic, not like the Americans. I mean, it is less prone to using violence."

He knew to take her comments seriously since one of her assets was her attention to details and research background.

"Do you think there is any connection to our activities?" he asked, forking a piece of bacon from the plate.

"No, I do not think so, but we must not dismiss the incident yet, after all, don't forget that there is the possibility that Agapov has sent some here and if so, then he is an unknown factor on the chessboard."

"Point taken," he said. "This is very good, by the way." He took another mouthful of the breakfast.

"*Spasibo,*" she said with a smile, setting the pot on the table and sitting down. "What is the plan for today?"

"I think it is time to push Comrade Wilcox. I do not like to have this go on much longer. I want to get what we need to finish our plans. Speaking of which, have you had any luck learning anything about our options here?"

"Apart from the information I gathered before leaving Ottawa, not a whole lot. It looks like there are several Consulates here but as far as I have been able to obtain, there is not a federal agency here we can contact. If we are committed to our plan to defect then we must consider the possibility that we will have to approach a country other than Canada, unless we decide to contact the RCMP or the military."

"I am not keen on the first option," he said, sitting back in his chair. "Too many leaks and there's no guarantee that they have not been infiltrated by the KGB. The second option would be a possibility, yes, provided we approach the right person. If I remember correctly, the highest-ranking military person here is an admiral. I think I will ask Wilcox to get us the names of anybody in intelligence of high enough rank. I believe we would have a better chance of success if we surrendered to them than anyone else."

"I agree," Ivanka said.

* * *

Josef Sokolov

Half an hour later, now dressed for the day ahead, Sokolov went to the phone and dialed.

"Mr. Wilcox, please," he said into the phone when it was answered at the other end.

"One moment," the voice said, then the line went dead.

"Lab, Wilcox speaking," Peter Wilcox said once connected.

"Ah, my friend. I'm in town for the day and thought I would like to get together with you for lunch; my treat."

"Hans, this is a surprise," Wilcox said easily, using Josef's alias. "Sure, why not. I can get away around noon. Where do you want to meet?"

"You choose."

"There's a diner on Gottingen Street serve's a pretty decent lunch." He gave him the name and address. "See you at noon."

"Noon," Sokolov said then hung up. He smiled at their little performance played out for the benefit of any listeners who might be monitoring calls to the facility.

"It's set for noon," he said, turning to Ivanka who was standing at a mirror on the wall, brushing her hair.

"I heard," she said. "I must visit a salon while we are here." This last statement was directed more at the image in the glass.

"Ah, the vanity of a woman."

She turned away and looked at him with a smile.

* * *

Peter Wilcox

Peter Wilcox hung up the phone and stole a quick, casual look around at the nearby desks to see if anyone was paying any attention to him. No one seemed to be showing any interest. He turned back to his work thinking he would be so much happier once the Russians were gone. He was for their cause, but he also knew he was not cut out for this spying business.

Twenty minutes later, his phone rang again.

"Lab, Wilcox," he said, a slight edge in his voice.

"Peter?" Caroline Simpson said in his ear.

"Caroline? I haven't heard from you in a while. What a nice surprise."

"Yeah, sorry about that, but I've been busy with my practice."

"That's okay. It's still, as always, great to hear from you. So, what's up?"

He had stayed in touch with her since graduating from university. He met her in one of his political science courses and became infatuated with her. It was through her that he was introduced to Communism and the Soviet Cause. Initially, he joined purely for the opportunity of starting an intimate relationship with her, but then became a believer. They did become lovers in time and still continued to share intimacies, although only frequently.

"Are you free to get together?"

"Absolutely," he said, somewhat eagerly thinking of her naked body. "When?"

"Today?"

There was something in her tone that suddenly dispelled any idea of a romp in the sack.

"Yeah, sure," he said, a hint of disappointment in his voice. "I'm meeting someone for lunch at noon but I can see you afterwards."

"Good. Let's meet up at my place after work. You remember where I live?"

"Yeah, see you then."

"And Peter...thanks."

"Bye," he said then hung up.

Her place. Maybe not all was lost, he thought, as he went back to his work.

Wilcox entered the diner and, once his eyes adjusted to the interior lighting, he spotted Sokolov sitting at a table in the corner with a mug of coffee in front of him. He made past a couple of empty tables with dirty dishes on them.

"Why the call?" he asked, pulling a chair out and sitting down.

"How are you coming along with those documents I asked for?" Sokolov asked without any preamble.

"I'm working on it. Like I told you already, those papers are kept in a secure area to which I don't have the proper clearance, but you knew this, so what else do you need?"

"You are a clever man. I like that. Yes, you are correct, there is something I need you find out for me."

Just then a cute waitress stepped up, holding a pot of coffee in her hand. She wore a white blouse and a skirt with an apron tied over the front. A small order pad protruded from the only pocket sewn on it. She automatically tilted the coffee pot over Sokolov's half empty mug.

"What'll you have?" she asked, looking at them as she set the pot down and took out the pad and a pencil from behind her ear.

"Ham and cheese sandwich; toasted with a pickle on the side and a coffee," Wilcox said. He noted that there was cream and sugar already on the table.

She jotted the order down, then looked at Sokolov.

"I think that would be fine for me as well," he said with a smile.

They both watched her, appreciating the view, as she walked away. They were both men after all.

"So? What else do you need?" Wilcox asked, leaning slightly forward.

"I need the names of the head of security here in the city. Preferably, military, but also RCMP. Can you get that information?"

"Easily, in fact, I can already give you their names. The military head is a Lieutenant Commander Jules Swanson. He's with the navy up at Stadacona. As far as I know he's actually with the British navy. There's another man connected with the army, but it's Swanson who runs all security on our projects. The civilian is an Inspector with the RCMP; his name is Bryon McKinnon; the two work together."

"Excellent. Write their names down here," he pulled out a small note pad and slid it across to him. "And their locations, if you know them."

Wilcox took the pad and, taking out a pen from inside his jacket, did as instructed.

"Mind if I ask why you need these?" he asked when he finished, pushing the pad back.

"Better for you not to know," Sokolov said, taking the pad and putting in his pocket. "But you will still try and obtain information, da?"

"Yes, I'll do what I can. Is that it?"

"Da. Now let us enjoy our meal," he said as he spotted the waitress approaching with two plates.

Later that afternoon, Wilcox was finishing up a series of computations when he noticed the time: four-forty-five. Time to pack it in for the day and to head over to Caroline Simpson's place.

She lived in a small bungalow style house she recently purchased not too far from Dalhousie on Beech Street, close to Jubilee Road. He had been there on a couple of occasions, spending the night when she was in the 'mood'. He did not mind that was as far as she wanted to take it with him since she was an exciting bedmate.

He arrived at her house a little after six, having stopped at his digs to change into fresher clothes. It was just starting to grow dark as evening was coming on and it was overcast. He parked his sports car in her driveway as he always did and got out. Just as he was about to ring the bell, the door opened, and there she stood.

Five-foot-five in her stocking feet and weighing a very nice one-ten, she was wearing a floral-patterned frock that hung down to her knees with a blue sash around her waist. She had a nice trim, fit body with perky breasts. When he looked at her, she was smiling.

"Thanks for coming," she said in a voice that always seemed to have a slight musical quality to it. "Come in." She stepped aside to let him pass.

"Always happy to see you," he said, leaning in and kissing her on the cheek. "I was a bit surprised when you called. It's been what...several months since our last time."

"I know; sorry, but it's been hectic at the practice and I'm usual late home and only want to sleep."

"That's okay," he said. "So?"

She led the way through to the living room. That's when he saw the man sitting on the large sofa. The first thing he sensed about him was something sinister, dangerous. He felt a slight chill run down his back.

"Peter, meet Comrade Pavlo Palyvoda," Caroline said as she took a seat on one of the stuffed chairs.

He walked over and offered his hand to the big Russian who accepted it with a firm grip.

"He has been sent here on an assignment for the KGB. I got a call from him asking for assistance, and earlier I had contact with someone in Ottawa telling me to assist him if he asked. Anyway, something has happened, and he now finds himself without a safe place to stay."

She said this as I moved away and took the other chair.

"And what does that have to do with me?" he asked without thinking, turning his eyes away from Palyvoda, fixing them on her.

"I was hoping you could help find a safe location where he could stay out of sight without drawing attention to himself?"

"What makes you think I would know such a thing?"

"I don't know, but I thought since you worked with the military you would know of, um, certain places. I assumed you know some of the sailors or where they hang out, that sort of thing."

Looking back at the Russian, Peter saw that he was staring him; his eyes hard, cold.

"What did he do?" Wilcox asked, not looking at her directly.

"I don't know, and to be honest, I don't want to know. I was told to help him, that's it. Now I'm asking you to help me. I know you are still loyal to the cause; it's why I called you. So? Will you help me?" she asked, her voice suddenly sounding urgent.

"Yes," he said. "Of course, I'll help. I just don't how much I can."

"Look. All he needs is a safe place. After that he's on his own; we're out of it."

Wilcox turned to Palyvoda and asked, "Do you speak English?"

"Yes," he said in a deep voice.

"Right. There are several hotels in and around the city where they don't ask any questions. Is a hotel okay with you?"

He nodded.

Turning back to Caroline, he asked, "Can he stay here until I can set something up?"

"For how long?" she asked.

"One night should do."

"Okay. One night. I owe you one," she said, as Wilcox stood up.

"And I plan to collect...soon," he said with a suggestive smile. "I best be going if I'm to fix something. I'll call you when I have something."

"Thanks, Peter," she said, standing up and following him out of the room.

"You will stay here for tonight. I have a spare room you can use. Do you want something to eat? I can make you something if you are hungry."

"Strong tea and some bread and cheese, if you have."

"I think there is something I can prepare." She turned and headed for the kitchen. She felt a little uneasy about him; nothing she could put her finger on exactly, but...something. It made her feel slightly very uneasy, and she did not like it.

Peter Wilcox left her house and got in is car feeling disappointed and a bit put out. He wasn't an operative, only a contact who sometimes passed on information. He didn't know the other side of Halifax; its underbelly, as it were. Sure, he knew about some of the places with questionable reputations like most other citizens but had never been to any of them.

As he headed back into the downtown area, he wondered how he was going to handle this. Something inside him seemed to be warning him that failure might have dangerous consequences, if he read Palyvoda correctly.

Four hours later, he returned to Simpson's house. Fifteen minutes after he went inside, he re-emerged with the Soviet agent behind him.

"Where are we going?" Palyvoda asked as he eased his bulk into the passenger side of the sports car.

"It is a hotel down on Hollis Street," Wilcox said, inserting the car key into the ignition. "It is not classy, in fact, just the opposite, but you'll fit in there and no one will ask any questions."

"Good. Many people there?"

"I don't know. From what I have heard, the operator runs a floating card game and some hookers there; maybe even sells liquor."

"How do you know this? You been there?"

"No. I called someone I know and was told that this place would be a good place to hide away from prying eyes."

"How much?"

"Thirty dollars a day."

"And the police? They watch this place?"

"I don't know," he said, manoeuvring the car up Jubilee Road, towards Oxford Street. "Possibly. It's the best I could do at short notice."

"It will do," Palyvoda said sounding like a grunt.

Wilcox suddenly became aware that he sweating, and his hands felt clammy on the leather steering wheel.

In point of fact, he did know something about the place he was taking Palyvoda from stories he heard in the mess hall. It was a rough place; fights were not uncommon, and the hookers were questionable. The owner was reputed to be a mobster down from Montreal. It all sounded like someplace out of an American gangster movie and just a bit exciting, but definitely not for him.

He took a quick sidelong glance at his passenger, thinking the man probably would feel right at home there. It did not matter to him once he got free of him. Peter looked ahead and pushed the small car a little faster.

Chapter Fourteen

Jesse Thompson

Friday the 13th. Good thing I'm not a superstitious sort.

I drove down Gottingen Street, heading for RCMP headquarters. I would park nearby and walk to the ferry for the crossing to Dartmouth. As I drove, I was thinking I would glad to see the back end of this assignment. It was turning into more than just finding the Soviet agents. Now it looked like there was another agent here; one who might be a killer, if Pete Duncan could tie him to a murdered woman. Fortunately, I was not involved with that investigation. It was Inspector McKinnon and Detective Pete Duncan's problem; at least as far as the killing was concerned. I could get dragged in if the killer did turn out to be a Soviet agent.

I could not waste time thinking about that at this time, I had other fish to fry. Carol managed to get me the particulars on Caroline Simpson yesterday. I decided that I would take a different tack with her by simply showing up at her office and interview her, catching her unawares, so to speak, and maybe off-guard. Worked for me many times before.

Her office was over in Dartmouth on Portland Street, not too far from the Dartmouth terminal. According to the information Carol gave me, Simpson passed the bar just after the war in nineteen-forty-seven. She worked for one of the established law firms in the city, but eventually left under a cloud. Seemed her politics did not sit well with her very conservative bosses. Looked like she was still a believer in the Soviet political view.

As I drove, a thought occurred to me: was she a Soviet 'sleeper', working for them off anyone's radar? If that was the case, then it was possible if the killer was another agent on the lam and needing help he might contact her. This raised another question. Why send an assassin here? Was it to deal with the other two?

I could see why the two agents sent already were here, but this third person...was he sent to assist them; spy on them, or kill them?

The KGB was notorious for its mistrust and compulsive need to maintain control over their own agents, especially those working abroad. This was something I learned dealing with them over the last couple of years. I supposed it was a direct reaction to the defection back in nineteen-forty-five by Igor Gouzenko which created a major breakdown of their North American spy networks.

But for now, my immediate concern was to find the other two agents and identify those working with them. To that end, I still needed to confront Peter Wilcox and this lawyer, Caroline Simpson.

The crossing was quite pleasant; the weather was comfortably warm for March, and the views of the city from the water were interesting. I noted the number of commercial ships that were berthed along the waterfront indicating the city was a major seaport on one of the world's busiest trade routes. Then there was the naval dock yard; I counted more than fifteen warships of various types. Seeing the city from this perspective explained why it still looked something out of a nineteen-forties war movie.

Portland Street began at the exit from the ferry. I walked up the block and a half to a small two-story wooden building with a women's dress shop on the main level. Next to the entrance I spotted the brass plate: C. Simpson, Barrister; 2nd Floor, embossed on it. I opened the door and headed up the stairs.

When I reached the frosted glass panelled door I did exactly what she had stencilled on the bottom right corner: I grabbed the doorknob and entered.

Inside was a small reception area with several wooden chairs and a desk with a young slightly effeminate looking man sitting behind it. There were two other people sitting in the waiting area: a man and woman. The man behind the desk looked up when I stepped in.

"Yes?" he said. "Do you have an appointment?"

I stepped up to the desk, taking out my identity wallet, I showed him my badge.

"Yes." I said, looking down at him.

"Oh. Just a moment, please." He reached for the phone on the desktop and depressed a button at the bottom, keeping his eyes fixed on me. "Sorry to interrupt you, but there's a rather large Mountie standing in front of me who says he has an appointment to see you, but I don't see any...oh...uh-huh, yes, right away," he said, then hung up.

"She is with a client at the moment and asks that you take a seat. She said she'll be ready for you in five minutes."

"Thank you," I said, removing my hat and taking one of the empty chairs, keeping my ID in my hand.

Seven minutes passed before the door to her inner office opened and an older woman and a young man emerged. I watched as they expressed their thanks then turned to leave.

Caroline Simpson was not what I expected to find.

She was tall, standing at five-five; she looked like she was in her early thirties with a slender figure, looking more like a ballet dancer than a lawyer. She had an attractive face framed by a head of almost jet-black hair that was cut very short. She wore a dark grey two-piece suit with a white blouse underneath. The only piece of apparel that cut into the masculine appearance was the pink silk scarf tied around her neck under the blouse's collar.

"You're the RCMP officer?" she said in a clear confident voice.

"Inspector Jesse Thompson," I said, standing up, offering my hand.

"May I see your identification?" She accepted my hand with a firm grip.

I passed her my wallet which she took and opened. After studying the ID card for a moment, she returned it to me.

"Why do want to talk to me?" she asked bluntly, but without any rancour.

"Can we discuss my visit inside," I said, gesturing to her inner office.

She took a backward step slightly to the side and I eased by her. I caught a whiff of her perfume which I realized was the same one Marie wore. We took our respective seats at her desk.

"I have been sent here to look into security matters at the naval facilities. Nothing special; just routine random spot checks," I started.

"And what does that to do with me exactly?"

"The checks involve personnel engaged on sensitive projects." I let that hang there for a moment let it sink in and see if it got any reaction. Nothing.

"Peter Wilcox," I continued. "Ring any bells?"

"No," she said. "Should it?"

"Yes. He and you were members of a pro-Soviet group while at university. According to our records, it seems you were a bit more than fellow flag wavers."

She sat there looking at me with a stony stare.

"Our records also point to the fact that you still maintain support for the Soviet Union."

"It's still my right to advocate for and support any political affiliation I choose."

"Absolutely," I said, keeping an even tone in my voice. "No one's suggesting otherwise. However, we do take an interest in citizens who may be possible agents for adversarial countries and who have demonstrated a propensity for spying and stealing our state secrets. And," I said, raising my hand as she began to say something, "we know that you still maintain a connection to Wilcox."

"So, you people have been spying on me, is that it?" she snapped.

I didn't say anything, letting her make her own assumptions.

"Are you here to investigate me...again?" she said, breaking the silence.

"Like I said, my interest is in checking out the people working for the government in sensitive areas, like Peter Wilcox. Are you saying that you and he are no longer in contact?"

"I don't have to answer such questions, so unless you have a warrant, or plan to detain me, this meeting is over."

"I guess I'll take that as a yes," I said, not moving.

"I don't care what you think," she snapped back. "Now if you don't mind, I have clients waiting."

I stood up and looking down at her said, "Thanks for your cooperation."

She just glared at me.

I turned and left the office. Back in my car, I sat behind the wheel, reviewing what just transpired upstairs. I was a bit puzzled by her reaction to my visit and the open hostility she demonstrated. It didn't make any sense; there wasn't any reason for her to act that way unless she was hiding something, or someone. According to our intelligence reports, the Soviets did not have an active presence here in the city, which in itself was odd given the work being done here. However, that did not mean that they didn't have other connections. The KGB has been known to work with many pro-Soviet groups not unlike the one she belonged to at college. They more, often than not, find members who are willing to 'assist' them without actually engaging in direct espionage.

I started the car and eased out into traffic, heading for RCMP Headquarters.

"Oh good, you're back," Carol said as I walked past her open office. She picked up some papers and followed me down to my work area.

"What's up?" I asked as we entered the room.

"Detective Duncan called," she said. "Wanted you to contact him when you came in. Also. Jules Swanson called. He wants you to call as well." She gave me a funny look.

"It's a curse. Being so popular an' all. Something I was born with, I guess."

"You seem to carry it easily enough," she said with a smile.

"Thanks, that it, no one else?"

"Nope, that's it, but hey, the day's still young. Coffee?"

"Yeah, thanks. Is Bryon in?"

"Uh-huh. Want me to let him know you're in?"

"No, that's okay, I'll just go along and drop in."

"Alright, I'll bring your coffee there?"

"Thanks."

I stepped aside as Carol left the room, followed her into the hall, then went on to Bryon McKinnon's office. I found him sitting at his desk behind what I was beginning to think was his usual condition: buried behind a stack of files.

"Morning," I said as I closed the door behind me and took a seat.

"Mornin'," he answered, closing a file and looking at me. "Carol tell you that Pete Duncan called?"

"Uh-huh. I'll be calling him back when we're done. Any idea what it's about?"

"One of his men thinks he might've picked up something. It was one of his men he assigned to keep an eye on Wilcox."

"Yeah...and?"

"Tailed him to an eatery yesterday 'round midday, where he thinks he saw him meet up with another man."

"That it? Didn't he go inside?" I asked.

"Apparently he was in his car when he saw them meet." He raised his eyebrows and shrugged. "Must've one of his new men. What about you, making any headway?"

I gave him the Reader's Digest view of my meeting with Caroline Simpson.

"Sounds like an angry woman," he said when I finished.

"I thought so. Although, I got the feeling there was something else going on."

"How so?'

"It struck me that her anger was a bit much. No; I think she's hiding something."

"Think she's a 'mole'?"

"Not if our intelligence is current. I was told when I was briefed before leaving Ottawa, that there was no evidence of any KGB operatives or operation here, despite the fact of the work being done here," I said.

"Yeah, that really had me puzzled too," he said.

The door opened just at that moment and Carol came in carrying a tray with two mugs of hot coffee and a plate with wafers on it. She set it on his desk, "Buzz if you want anymore," she said, looking back from the door, then was gone.

"Yeah, I've been wondering about it to. Simpson could've been recruited as a resource, or as what the Yanks are calling, an asset. Someone to call on for assistance or information without using them as actual agents," I said.

"Good point. So, you think she might somehow be tied into these two agents you're looking for, possibly even this third agent; the suspected killer of that old woman?"

"All possibilities," I said, taking a sip of the coffee.

"How do you want to proceed? We can't arrest her; no grounds."

"I know," I said, setting the mug down on the desk. "I can always have her picked up under the security regulations. No warrant necessary."

"And we can detain her almost indefinitely," Bryon said.

"But then we'd lose any chance of catching any of the others. No; I think we let her continue on, but under surveillance from our men."

"That could be a problem. This detachment is undermanned at the moment."

"How many can you spare?"

"Four. Tops. What about using some of Swanson's people? He's got a stake in this as well?"

"Funny you should mention him. Carol said he called looking for me as well. I'll discuss this with him when I call him back, unless you want to coordinate with him?"

"Yeah, I think that'd probably work better since this will involve both our departments."

"Okay, I'll let him know you'll be getting in touch. Anything else?"

"Not much," he said. "We did confirm that the lawyer Captain Carew visited is definitely part of the homosexual community. Apparently, there was an incident a while back involving an assault on a citizen suspected of interfering with a minor; a young man, a teenager, and he was the council for the plaintiff. His, er, inclinations came to light at the time."

"Still circumstantial," I said. "But definitely damning all the same."

"It's in the file I'm putting together to pass on to Swanson when you're done."

"Hmmm. If that's it, then I best return those calls. I'll hook up with you later."

"Right."

I got up and left his office, thanking Carol for the coffee as I stepped past her desk.

Back at my desk, I reached for the phone and dialed Pete Duncan's number.

"Detective Duncan," he said when he picked up.

"Morning, Pete, it's Jesse," I said. "You called."

"Mornin'. Yeah. One of my guys I put on your man Wilcox, reported tailin' him to a diner where he was seen meeting another man."

"I know, McKinnon just filled me in. Too bad he didn't get a chance to go inside."

"He's new to the job. I already spoke to him. Anyway, he stayed on him when he came out, but then packed it in after he returned to work. He went back later and picked him up again. Seems he paid a visit to someone down the south end of town. I checked the directory for the address an' guess who lives there?"

"Caroline Simpson," I said, taking a stab in the dark.

"Not bad," Pete said, sounding impressed. "You're right. I'm guessin' this is important."

"Yeah, it is." I quickly filled him in on the connection.

"So, if she's a 'Red' the maybe she's involved with these agents?"

"My gut reaction is yeah; I believe she might be."

"That'd mean she could also be connected to the killin'."

"Maybe," I said. "Assuming the killer was this third agent. I think her involvement is limited though, most likely as a support resource."

"So, she could be helpin' this agent by hidin' him out?"

"Maybe, but not directly. If she is doing anything she'd be using someone else to help her."

"Peter Wilcox?"

"That'd be my guess, yeah. Might explain why he went to her home. Coincidence? I'm not sure."

"This guy would need to find a new hole to hide in, right? My money'd be on him settin' up a new place where he could operate from."

"Good point," I said. "Let me guess, you just happen to know about such places here in town?"

"You could say that," he said, chuckling. "I'll start nosin' around. I know some people I can call, an' get back to you. I think I'll put a tail on this Simpson woman as well, you never know."

"Don't bother, I'll get Bryon to put a man on her."

"Okay, thanks."

The line went dead. I immediately dialed Jules Swanson's number.

"Lieutenant Commander Swanson's office," a sweet voiced woman said.

"Good morning," I said. "This is Inspector Thompson with the RCMP. I am returning his call."

"Oh, yes, Inspector. Unfortunately, he is not here at the moment. He has been called to Admiralty House; however, I expect him back within the hour. Is there a number he can reach you?"

"If it's all the same, I would prefer to have a face to face with him."

"Let me check his schedule for today, one moment." I heard a soft thud as she laid the phone down. A moment later she was back.

"He's got a clear spot at two o'clock," she said.

"That works," I said. "I'll be there at two, thanks."

"All set, see you when you arrive."

"Bye," I said then hung up.

I checked my watch: eleven-forty-five. It was close enough to lunch time and I realized I was hungry, not having eaten anything since seven this morning. I rang Bryon's number, and we agreed to go for a bite to eat up at the Green Lantern Building diner on Barrington Street. It was a short ten-minute walk from here and it was not too bad a day outside. Before leaving, I wrote a quick reminder to myself on the pad to check in with Ottawa and the love of my life.

Chapter Fifteen

Jesse Thompson

I arrived at Stadacona at one-fifty for my meeting with Jules Swanson. After going through the routine of passing through the gate, I drove to his building and found a place to park. When I reached his office, his secretary waved me in, asking if she could bring me a coffee or tea. I opted for a coffee.

"Ah, Jesse," Jules Swanson said in his usual jovial voice. "So good of you to come up. Take a pew." He gestured to one of the nearby chairs. "Coffee?"

"Already taken care of, thanks," I said, sitting down.

"Excellent. How is your investigation progressing?"

"It's moving along. I've managed to narrow it down to just one of those names I gave you, Peter Wilcox. In addition, I think I may have uncovered a sleeper, someone sympathetic to their political agenda. A local barrister named Caroline Simpson. We have put her under surveillance for now. I was told you called?"

"Yes, I was curious to know where we stood at the moment."

"Sorry, about that," I said, as the door opened, and a WAVE came in carrying a small tray with two mugs and decanters of cream and sugar. She set it on the corner of the desk then left without a word.

"We've been a bit busy," I said, continuing my statement.

"I know," he said, reaching for one of the mugs. "I heard about that poor woman. Throat cut, as I understand it. Nasty business that. Any progress on the who the killer might be?"

"There's a distinct possibility that it might have been a third Soviet agent who may have been sent here to watchdog the other two."

"I don't understand. Why would he want to kill an old woman?"

"Apparently, she ran a boarding house and was something of a busy body, liked poking into other people's business. If this agent was a boarder and caught her nosing around..."

"Yes, I see. I assume the local police are involved in the matter?"

"Uh-huh, A Detective Pete Duncan; a good man by all accounts and he has a history working with naval intelligence during the war."

"I know the name. You say that you have excluded the other two names from your list, does that mean they are cleared?"

"For the most part as it relates to my investigation, yes, however, I would advise that your office take a deeper look at Captain Carew. We have uncovered strong circumstantial evidence that he may be an active homosexual. Bryon McKinnon is compiling a file on him which he will turn over to you for further action."

"Hmmm. We have had our suspicions about him for a while but decided to take a watch and see approach for the time being. However, if you have something, we will have reconsider our handling of the matter."

"Have you been able to garner any more information on those missing papers from your records department?" I asked, picking up my mug.

"It does seem to be the case that Peter Wilcox was the last person to sign in at the time of the discovery. However, we cannot definitely place him in the restricted area. We are currently reviewing the security systems used there and looking for ways to better monitor who accesses the area, specifically, we are installing the new closed circuit camera system. It's due here in the next few days. In fact, we intend to install them throughout the base and dockyard."

"Good to hear," I said. "By all accounts it's a good system."

"Now, about Wilcox?"

'Yes?"

"Are you ready to turn him over to me yet?"

"No. He's my only link to finding the two Soviet agents. I'm convinced he knows where they are and is working with them. If you intervene at this point, I'm afraid they'll go to ground even deeper. Besides, this may just be the tip of the iceberg. There may be others."

"That's a worrying thought," Swanson said. "Alright, I will stay back…for now, but I have to insist that my department monitor him, surreptitiously, of course."

"Agreed. Thanks. I think from this day onward any contact between our offices should be between you and Bryon, if that works for you? I really need to concentrate on finding these agents now and these other matters, though possibly related, are proving to be a distraction. And could end up being detrimental."

"I understand," he said, "and, yes, have Bryon contact me, and we will work out the details. And, Jesse, good hunting."

"Thanks."

We stood up and shook hands, then I headed back to my car. I decided that as the day was getting on, I would call it a day and headed for my billet.

* * *

Peter Wilcox

Around the same time as Jesse was meeting with Swanson, Peter Wilcox stepped into the phone booth located on the corner across from the main gate and closed the glass panelled door. He inserted the nickel required to make a call and dialed.

"Hello," Ivanka Chenko said in his ear. This was the first time he had heard her voice, since he never met her with her, always meeting with Sokolov alone.

"This is Peter Wilcox," he said.

"One moment."

"Comrade," Sokolov said a moment later. "You have something?"

"Yes. I gave you those names at the diner, but here's a bit more information and another name you should be aware of."

"Da. Very good. Wait while I get a pen and paper." then, a moment later he was back. "Proceed."

"The man heading up security at the base is Lieutenant Commander Jules Swanson. He's with the British navy. The other name is an Inspector Bryon McKinnon. He's with the RCMP and works with Swanson on security matters, according to my source. The other person you should know about is another Mountie: Inspector Jesse Thompson. I hear he is with their intelligence division in Ottawa."

"Excellent," Sokolov said. "This is most helpful. Have you managed to get any further with obtaining what I have asked for?"

"Not yet," Wilcox said. "It looks like something's going on at the records room. Some kind of security shake up. I think it might have something to do with those papers I already got for you."

"Most unfortunate."

"I don't think I should take a chance on going there again," he said, sounding nervous. "It's too risky."

"I agree, you should not expose yourself. I will consider other options. You have been a good and loyal ally. We may talk again. Be careful."

Then the line went dead.

He hung up and stepped out of the booth with a feeling of relief, thinking that it wasa finally over. He could go back to his regular life again without the nagging fears of being caught.

* * *

Josef Sokolov

"Has something happened?" Ivanka asked, looking at him from where she sat.

"I think our mission here may be compromised," he said, moving to the other chair and sitting down.

"Oh?"

"He did manage to obtain the names of two people we can contact: both in their security community. However, one is a British naval officer."

"That is a problem?" she asked.

"You know as I do, how deeply the GRU has penetrated the British government. I think we must be careful."

"So, it is time then?" she asked.

"I think so. Unfortunately, we do not have enough insurance, as they say, to ensure they will accept us."

"There are always the names of the people working for the KGB," she said. "And there is also what we know."

"I know. It is just that while I have no issues with sharing information on our spy-craft; I hate the feeling that we are betraying Mother Russia. I do not think I can give them any information which would endanger my country."

"I know, my love," she said in a soft, tender voice. She stood up and went to him, wrapping her arms around his head which she held it tenderly against her breasts. "I know."

Just then the phone rang. He eased himself free and went to answer it.

"Hello," he said when he picked up the receiver.

"You have not reported in for two days, is something wrong?" Sergi Agapov asked in a demanding voice.

"*Nyet*. No, nothing is wrong. There has not been anything to report," Sokolov said, testily.

"Do I detect a tone of recrimination? I told you to report whether you had new information or not."

"No. It is proving difficult to obtain the information you sent us down here for. Our contact has reported that the security is exceptionally tight and that they are changing their procedures in light of his last document procurement, which you are aware of."

"Are you saying that the mission is at risk of exposure?" he asked.

"I cannot say for certain, but he has indicated that an RCMP intelligence agent has recently arrived from Ottawa. Unexpected," Sokolov said, "how do want us to proceed?"

"Your mission remains the same," Agapov said. "That information is vital."

"Understood. We will continue to try and obtain it."

"Good. And Sokolov, do not disobey my orders again. You will report to me daily, is that clear?"

"Da, Comrade."

The line went dead. Sokolov slowly hung up the receiver. He stood there for a moment longer, letting the rising anger he felt inside him subside. Their time was running out.

Moments after the call, the desk clerk disconnected the line and then dialed the number to the police department.

"Halifax Police," a voice said after two rings.

"I want to speak to Detective Wallace, please," he said.

"Just a moment."

195

"Detective Wallace."

"Hey, Wally, it's me Frank at the Waverley."

"What's up?" the detective asked.

"'Member you asked me to keep an eye an' open on them foreigners stayin' here?"

"Yeah, why, ya got somethin'?"

"Maybe. They just got a long-distance call from Ottawa. Anyway, I know you're interested in somethin' like this, so I plugged in an' listened."

"Okay, an'...?"

"Not a lot really, jus' stuff 'bout a mission or somethin' and wantin' some information pretty bad, oh yeah, an' they called each other comrade."

"That's it?'

"Uh-huh," Frank said.

"Okay. I owe ya one. Thanks."

"Anytime."

Detective Wallace hung up his phone, stood up and went over to Pete Duncan's desk.

"I jus' got off the horn with Frank Henry, he's one a' the desk clerks at the Waverley, that's where some foreigners are registered. Anyway, accordin' to him, one a' them jus' got a long-distance call from somebody in Ottawa. He heard them talkin' about some sort a' mission an' information they needed. He also heard them say the word 'comrade'."

"Did he say which one got the call," Pete asked, turning in his chair and looking up at his colleague.

"No, I didn't think to ask," Wallace said, a bit abashedly. "I'll call back an' ask him."

"Do that an' then let me know, an' George, thanks. Good work."

Pete watched the young detective walk back to his desk then reached for his phone. A moment later a woman answered.

"This is Detective Duncan at police headquarters, is Jesse Thompson in?" he asked.

"No, sorry," she said. "He went out earlier. I suspect you can reach him up at the officer's quarters at Stad. He's billeted there. Here's the number." She recited the five-digit number, and he wrote it down.

"Thanks," he said, "I don't suppose Inspector McKinnon is in?"

"Yes he is, want me to transfer you?"

"Yeah, thanks."

A moment later, "Pete. How're you doin'?" McKinnon said.

"Okay. Listen, one a' my men jus' got a call from one of his informants, a clerk at the Waverley. You're aware that there're some foreigners stayin' there. Anyway, seems one of them received a call from someone in Ottawa an' was heard talkin' about a mission an' important information. He also reported hearing them use the word, 'comrade'."

"Interesting," McKinnon said. "Did he get a name?"

"He's gettin' it now. Sounds like we might 'a found Jesse's spies?" Pete said. "Hold on a sec."

197

He moved the phone receiver away from his ear as Wallace came back.

"It's man and woman; registered as Mr. and Mrs. Maas from Belgium, he thinks," Wallace said, dropping the handwritten note on the desk.

"Thanks," Pete said, putting phone back to his ear and picking up the note.

"They're registered as Mr. And Mrs. Maas supposedly from Belgium," he said into the mouthpiece. "Whaddya want to do now?"

"Let's wait until we have a chance to speak with Jesse before we act. If these are the people, he's lookin' for, then there's a bigger picture to consider."

"Politics?"

"Don't think so, at least not directly. Jesse's hoping to throw a wider net and maybe catch a lot more people."

"Okay. Let me know when an' where. I'll be here for another coupla hours."

"Right," McKinnon said. "Oh, by the way, how're you makin' out on the dead woman case?'

"It's startin' to look like we're dealin' with the other agent you guys suspect is here. We did a check of some of the local boozers an' learned that there was a foreigner seen drinkin' there in the last coupla days. No one knew who he was or where he came from but one a them's pretty sure the guy sounded like a Russian. Apparently, he's a stevedore an' has worked a few Russian ships towards the end of the war."

"That's somethin'" Byron said. "Jesse'll be glad to hear it. I don't suppose you were able to make any connection to the dead woman?"

"Not that lucky," Pete said. "Although, she was known to some a people there."

"Okay, Good work to you an' your men. I'll pass this on to Jesse when I see him. Thanks."

"No problem, later," Pete said then the line went dead.

Chapter Sixteen

Jesse Thompson

"Jesse?" Byron called out as I walked past his office the next morning. "Got a minute?"

I stopped and went inside.

"Morning," I said, sitting down. "What's up?"

"Got a call from Pete Duncan late yesterday," he began. "Looks like we caught a break. Remember the last report stating that there were five foreigners booked in at the Waverley Inn?"

I nodded.

"Well, one of his men's informants; a clerk at the Inn, contacted him. Seems that there was a long-distance call from Ottawa to a couple registered under the name of Maas. Anyway, the short of it is, this guy listened in on the call from the switchboard and claims he heard them talking about needing important information and something about a mission. He also said he heard them use the word comrade a coupla times. Think this is enough to identify this Maas couple as your agents?"

"It's a definite possibility," I said. "I wonder if they used passports when they registered?"

"Is that important?"

"Not sure. I was just thinking out loud. Did Pete leave the name of this clerk?"

"No. I can get it, why, you thinking about going there?"

"Thought I would, yeah. These people have to be checked out. I'll call Pete myself, besides I might want to have a quick chat with his man for a bit of background."

"Okay, I'll leave it to you," he said. "Good luck."

"Thanks," I said, standing up and heading to my office.

Okay, I thought, as I reached my work area; time to end this business. Now that I had a strong enough lead to the agents, I was sent here to stop I didn't think I could put off confronting them much longer. There was no way of knowing how much had been passed on already. First, though, I needed to talk with the hotel clerk. I picked up the phone and dialed Pete Duncan's number.

"Detective Duncan," he said when he answered.

"Hi Pete, it's Jesse Thompson," I said.

"Been expectin' to hear from you. I'm guessin' Bryon filled you in on those two foreigners at the Waverley?"

"Good guess, yeah. What I need is the name of your man's contact; the desk clerk who called it in."

"Yeah, okay, jus' a sec." I heard the phone as it hit his desk. He was back a few minutes later.

"You plannin' on havin' a talk with him?" he asked when he came back on the line.

"Something like that, yeah, why, that a problem?"

"Not for me, but I was plannin' on havin' a talk with him myself."

"Tell you what, let's hook up and see him together," I suggested.

"Works for me," Pete said. "Why don't I pick you up out front a' your building, say, in twenty minutes?"

"See you then." I hung up.

I was standing outside on the sidewalk when Pete rolled to a stop beside the curb to the sound of several angry motorists and a lorry driver who had to try and slip past him. I stepped off the curb and eased my way around to the passenger's side and carefully got in.

"Noisy drivers," I said.

"Whatever," he shrugged as he signalled and pulled away into traffic. "How do want to handle this when we get there?"

"I want to get as much information on this couple as I can before making my move; maybe even get a look in their room if they're out."

"Without a warrant?"

"Is that a problem for you?" I asked.

"Not really," he said, slowing for a traffic stop.

"Don't worry. There'll be no comeback on you. I'm operating under the authority granted by the National Secrets Act."

"Which covers a whole host of sins," he said sarcastically.

"Yes; it does, but necessary sins. So, what do know about this desk clerk?"

"His name is Frank Henry. Been workin' there a while. He's been a good source of reliable information from time to time. I called ahead to let him know we were comin' down."

We arrived at the Waverley at ten-forty-five. Pete pulled the car into the parking area on the left side of the wooden building.

The building was a large two story converted Victorian house; according to the plaque on the wall, built in eighteen-sixty-five. There was, what looked like an extension, added on the rear. If I had to guess, I would say it was originally one of the city's older private homes that had undergone changes since it was built. The inside more or less supported the impression. A wide stairway with a wooden banister on one side led to the second floor as you entered the ornate foyer which had a pineapple inlaid into the wooden floor, and a crystal chandelier overhead. Another fine example of Halifax's ties to its European heritage, I couldn't help thinking as we stepped over to the check-in desk. A thin older man sat behind it. He was short, maybe five-feet-two with a balding head.

"Hiya Pete," he said in a raspy voice. "Been awhile. How ya doin'?"

Must be a heavy smoker, I thought.

"Hi Frank. Good, thanks," Pete said. "This here is Inspector Thompson with the RCMP. He's interested in certain guests stayin' here."

"The ones I tole Wally 'bout, right?"

"Right. Let's go someplace where we can talk in private."

"Yeah, sure. Step 'round the counter an' let's go into the office. I gotta keep an eye on the desk, see; I'm on my own 'til noon when Jenny comes in."

Once inside, he went to the desk and sat down, facing the door.

"Tell me what you know about the Maas couple," I said.

"Not much to tell, really," Frank began. "Quiet sort, ya know? Keep pretty much to themselves. Don't even eat much here. They're not stand-offish, mind, but like I said, like to keep to themselves. Most they ever ask for is directions, usually to a restaurant or some other places."

"So why did you decided to call the police?"

"Well, Wally, he came in one day askin' if I knew 'bout any foreigners comin' in for rooms. That's when I tole him 'bout the few that're here. He asked me to keep an eye an' ear open, see, an' ta call if anythn' suspicious-like happened."

"I see," I said. "That's why you eavesdropped on the phone call?"

"Yeah, I suppose so, I mean, I don't usually do that, but he said..."

"We get it, Frank," Pete said, seeing that the old man was looking nervous. "You're not in any trouble, so relax. You did okay."

"Thanks, Pete, 'preciate that. Was only tryin' ta help."

"Are they in their room now?" I asked.

"No. They went out an hour ago," he said, looking back at me.

"They say where they were going or when they would be back?"

"Nope," he said, shaking his head.

"Let me have the passkey," Pete said. "What room?"

"Six. Upstairs near da back, right-hand side. Ya sure I won't get inta any trouble? I mean, ya don't have a warrant an' all, right?"

"We'll only be in there five minutes. Don't worry, you're safe."

He got up and went back to the front desk with us behind him. He reached for a key hanging on a board and picked one off.

"If you see them comin' back," Pete said, taking the key, "ring the room an' hang up after the first ring, got it?"

"Got it," Frank said as Pete led the way upstairs.

Once we reached room six, Pete stopped and looked me.

"I hafta say, I'm not real sure 'bout this."

"What?" I asked.

"This could be considered illegal, ya know. No warrant an' all."

"Look, you're here in case there's something that falls under your jurisdiction, as for entering their room without a warrant, that's covered by me being here. Like I told you before, we have a lot of latitude under the National Secrecy Act, and this is part of an intelligence investigation. But if you're uncomfortable I'll go in alone."

"No, that's okay. I was jus' being a cop; let's go," he said with a smile.

He inserted the key, and we went inside. It was the first time I saw a hotel room like this one. There was a large wood framed bed, two stuffed chairs and a sofa, all covered with heavy embroidered fabric. There was also a small table with an electric hot plate on it.

"Amazing," I said. "This must've been some home in its day."

"Yeah, well, let's get to work. I don't want to stay in here any longer than necessary.

We set about looking through everything: closets, bureaus, even the bathroom. Nothing, which did not surprise me.

"Hey," Pete said, "lookit this."

He was standing over a small wastebasket beside the table. I joined him and looked down. I saw scraps of partially burnt paper among a couple napkins. They were obviously once a sheet of note paper.

Pete bent down and fingered through them, pulling out a few pieces with writing on them.

"Whaddya make of this?" he asked showing me the markings. "I might be wrong but, don't that look like a part of McKinnon's name?"

I took the scrap of paper and clearly read the letters, 'innon'.

He passed me another piece. I saw the letters 'pson' written on it.

"You thinkin' the same me?"

"Looks like they know about Bryon and...me," I said. "If so, then how and why? Makes no sense."

"Well, it's really sketchy but, I think we gotta think they know. Too dangerous not to."

"Yeah," I said. "Let's grab all the pieces and see if we can put the page back together."

Pete collected as many of the scraps as he could with any markings still visible on them and put them in his shirt pocket. When finished, we headed for the door.

Later back at headquarters, Pete, Bryon and myself were huddled over the large table in the meeting room, trying to put the pieces together. After fifteen minutes, the best we could discern was the note definitely had at least three names on it. On one we found the letters, 'Ins' which we assumed was likely the word Inspector. We also found three pieces with the letters, 'Ju', w, on, on them. It was

Bryon who suggested the name might be Jules Swanson.

"Whaddya think it means?" Pete asked as we sat down, mulling over this discovery.

"If in fact, these are the names we're assuming, then it's even more confusing than we know," Bryon said.

"How so?" Pete asked.

"These are the names of the people working in security and intelligence.," I said. "Specifically, on the case I'm working."

Bryon nodded, adding, "What I don't understand is if they know about us why are they still at the Waverley? I mean, they'd have assume we're onto them, right?"

"Not necessarily," I said. "Think about it. We found these scraps today, which means they had to have received that note sometime in the last twenty-four maybe thirty hours."

"So?" Pete asked.

"Pete, didn't you tell me one of your men followed Peter Wilcox and saw him meet another man?"

"Yeah, so?"

"It's a distinct possibility that the man he met might've been one of the two staying in that room."

"Wilcox passed on the names?" Bryon said.

"Would makes sense; think about it. He would know that we're actively running security checks."

"Yeah, but how would he know about me, I'm more or less in the background on this investigation. Jules Swanson and you, maybe."

"I didn't say I had an explanation just that it fits," I said. "You know, something else could be going on here that is not part of why they're here."

"What?" Pete asked.

"That's the question," I said.

"So, now what?" he added.

"I think we have to pull Wilcox in," I said.

"I agree," McKinnon said. "It's time to shut this investigation down."

"That's all well an' good," Pete said. "But, what about this other agent; the one we think might've killed that woman?"

"I haven't forgotten him," I said. "I'm ready to help you find and capture this man."

"So am I," Bryon added.

"But don't forget, we still aren't sure there is a third man nor do we any evidence, that if there is, he's the one who killed her," I added. "I got a feeling that if he is here, then he's part of this business with the two agents somehow."

"You think these other two, Wilcox an' Simpson, might know somethin'?"

"A possibility, yes."

"Then you gonna pick her up as well?"

"Yes, I think so," I said. "However, I have to tell you that you won't be in on the detention."

"Oh? An' why's that?"

"Because I'm not officially arresting them. I don't have the authority or evidence to make any sort of charge. I do, however, have the authority as an intelligence officer to take them into custody and detain them without a charge under..."

"...the National Secrets Act," Pete said, cutting me off and finishing my statement.

I nodded.

"Christ, that's some sorta power you people have."

"The times we live in now, I'm afraid," I said. "Rest assured, if we shake anything of use to your investigation, we'll be only too happy to pass it along. You okay with that?" Bryon asked.

"Have to be," Pete said, "but I get it. If that's it, I think I best be gettin' back to the station. Good luck."

He stood and picked up his coat and headed out of the room.

"There goes a good cop," I said as the door closed.

"Yeah," Bryon said.

* * *

Josef Sokolov

"This is nice," Ivanka Chenko said, as she held onto Sokolov's arm.

It was a sunny morning, and the air was fresh with a gentle breeze on their faces. A perfect day for a walk in the Public Gardens; a small botanical treasure in the heart of Halifax. Luckily, it was mostly empty at this time of the day since many were at work or attending classes at one of the three universities.

They walked leisurely on the gravel path towards a large pond with a pair of swans in it. He led them to an empty wooden bench and sat down.

"I think it is time," he said, speaking quietly in Russian. "I do not feel good about continuing with the assignment. Your thoughts?"

"I go wherever you go, you know that," she said, watching the pair of white birds slowly swim by.

"Good. Then that's settled. Now, the only questions are how we make our move and who do we contact?"

"What did you say our choices were?"

"Either the head of naval intelligence; a British naval officer, or a senior policeman with the Royal Canadian Mounted Police who is supposedly connected to the intelligence community."

"I do not trust the British. Any move we make through him would be reported back to MI5 or Special Branch and we both know how they have been penetrated. Earlier I favoured the military, but I've changed my mind."

"Good point," he said. "That leaves the RCMP."

"There is no one else?"

Sokolov shook his head, "*Nyet*. There are very few embassies in the city, so that option is dubious at best."

"The RCMP then," she said with a note of finality.

"Agreed. Now, we must prepare what we will offer as trade for their cooperation and asylum. They will want as much information as possible, most likely, on our network of agents."

"I don't see a problem with giving them whatever they require, do you?"

"Not really, although, it is one thing to betray my country and another to betray people we have known for some time."

"I understand that, but these people still serve a government that no longer practices the principles or ideals of Communism. And do not forget; we know many of them would not hesitate to turn us over to the GRU if they even suspected what we are about to do. Remember Agapov."

"You are right, of course," he said, putting an arm over her shoulders. "Then, it is decided, da?"

"Da."

They sat for another twenty minutes enjoying the morning, each thinking of the new life that awaited them if everything went as planned.

Later that evening, back in their room, the phone rang.

"Hello?" Sokolov asked tentatively when he picked up the receiver.

"This is the front desk," a woman's voice said. "There's a long-distance call for Mrs. Maas."

"One moment," he said, putting a hand over the mouthpiece and holding the receiver out to Ivanka. "It's for you. Long distance."

She came over and took the phone, placing against her face.

"Hello?" she said.

"One moment, please." Then, a moment later.

"Ivanka?" a woman asked.

"Anya?"

"Yes. It's me. I need to talk to you. You are in danger; you and Josef."

"What do you mean?"

"I just received documents authorizing cash disbursements and travel papers for Pavlo Palyvoda to travel to Halifax. They were issued the same day as yours. I remembered that you and Josef were ordered there on an assignment. The authorization came from Comrade Agapov."

"I don't understand what...," Ivanka started to say.

"We have heard that Palyvoda is usually sent out when someone is to be terminated. I know there have been suspicions and rumours circulating through the embassy

213

about personnel and even some agents who may have become disaffected. You remember when they suddenly sent three clerks back to Moscow; that was Agapov's doing."

"And you think Palyvoda has been sent here to deal with us?"

"I don't know for certain," Anya said. "But I thought you should know. We go way back, and you have always been a good friend."

"*Spasiba*. We will be careful. Goodbye."

"What was that all about?" Sokolov asked when she hung up.

"You remember Anya Putin, the woman working in the cypher section? We were students at the technical college together. It looks like your concerns about Agapov being suspicious of us may be well-founded. It appears he has sent another agent here; an assassin, according to her, which could only mean he plans to take action against us. But why now? Do you think he knows of our plans to defect?"

"I don't know how he could, but then again, he does not need to know. He is a bastard; a dangerously ambitious bastard who thinks a few purges within the agency would serve his goals."

"Have you heard of this agent, Pavlo Palyvoda?" she asked.

"I have heard the name before but is all. It was linked to a highly secret section within the GRU."

"So, what do we do now?"

"Find him before he finds us."

"Then?"

He just stood there looking into her eyes and she knew.

They did not notice the man sitting on a bench on to the other side of the pond, apparently feeding a flock of pigeons at his feet.

* * *

Pavlo Playvoda

Pavlo Palyvoda left his room on Hollis Street shortly after checking in and headed for the Waverley Inn a few blocks away. It was not easy finding a discrete location to watch the entrance which annoyed him. He was forced to take up a post a half block away that afforded him a fairly good view of the steps while remaining out of sight. He knew it was a long shot, watching the Inn, not knowing if they were even inside, but he was used it. The only time he moved away was to cross over the street to the small store on the other side where he purchased several bags of nuts to snack on. An hour or so later, his patience was rewarded; Sokolov and the woman, Chenko, appeared on the steps. They stood there for a moment, looking around then descended to the sidewalk.

He watched, as they walked towards Morris Street, where they turned the corner and headed up the sloping street. He waited for several minutes then stepped out of his hiding place and followed behind them.

Fifteen minutes later, he followed them into the Public Gardens, a small botanical park in the heart of the city. When he saw them head for a bench facing a small pond, he changed direction and went to a vacant bench on the opposite side.

Something about their actions or maybe their apparent inactivity regarding their assignment seemed to bother him. It was time to report in for further instructions. He needed to find a secure phone; that meant a public payphone.

He stood up and walked back towards the gate he came in.

* * *

Josef Sokolov

"Do you see that man?" Ivanka asked without pointing or looking directly at the man on the bench on the other side.

"What man?" Sokolov said.

"Over there, on the other side."

He stole a quick casual glance. "What about him?"

"He seems familiar."

"Familiar? How?"

216

"I don't know, but I think maybe I have seen him before. Remember, I told you the other day that I thought I was being followed."

He glanced at him again, trying to make out any distinguishing features, but missed his chance as the man stood up and walked away. Josef thought he had seen enough to remember him.

"You think he might be this Palyvoda Anya warned me about?" she asked as she too, watched him walk off.

"I think we have to assume so," Sokolov said. "Too dangerous not to."

"I'm scared," she said, instinctively moving a bit closer to him.

"You stay here for ten minutes then return to our room. I will follow him and see what I can learn."

"Is that a good idea?"

"It should be okay, it's daytime, and the streets are crowded. I will be careful; do not worry."

"Alright."

"You have your pistol?"

"Da," she said, patting her handbag slung over her shoulder.

He leaned down and kissed her on the cheek then stood up, stepping towards the gate. Palyvoda was about sixty feet ahead of him and was about to exit the park onto the street. He stopped at the corner of Spring Garden Road and South Park Street waiting for a break in the traffic before stepping off.

Sokolov watched him from just inside the large wrought iron black gate not moving until the man was across the street. He was about to step out when he saw his quarry head for the entrance to the Lord Nelson Hotel. What was he up to, he wondered as he headed for the street just as Palyvoda went up the steps and went inside.

A few minutes later, Sokolov went to the steps and up to the door where a uniformed doorman held one side open for him. Inside, he looked around the ornate lobby. He saw his man just as he entered a glass panelled phone booth. He quickly turned around and headed back to the sidewalk, looking for a vantage point where could see the door without drawing attention to himself then settled in to wait.

Chapter Seventeen

Jesse Thompson

At the end of the meeting with Pete Duncan and Byron McKinnon, I called Ottawa to bring my boss up speed on the status of my investigation.

"DS Warton's office," Marie said in my ear, sending, as it always did, a soft shiver down my back.

"Hi baby," I said.

"Well, it's about time." I could almost picture that cute little pout she put on when she was annoyed with me.

"Now, now, be nice."

"Ooo, you. Why can't I stay mad at you?"

"We both know the answer to that question," I said with a not too subtle suggestive hint in my voice.

"Now who's being bad?"

"Is he in?" I changed the subject, since I was down here and she so far away.

"Yes, but don't go away when you're finished, okay?"

"You have to ask?"

The line went quiet for a few moments then I heard Warton's voice.

"How goes it?" he asked bluntly; his usual manner of speaking.

"I'm about ready to wrap this up," I said, giving him a full rundown on the situation thus far, adding that in my opinion, the security situation here with regards to the secret work being done was in good hands with Lieutenant Commander Swanson at the helm in spite of the unusual procedures in place. As for the reported Soviet agents, I told him we were closing in on them and would probably have them in custody within twenty-four hours.

"Good work, as usual," he said. "So, I guess we can expect to see you here by Monday?"

"If all goes to plan, yes sir," I said.

"Excellent. There'll be a well-deserved week off waiting for you."

"Thanks, and...?"

"Yes, I can spare her for a week."

"Thanks, again. I'll call before I leave."

"Alright. Now return the favour and don't keep her on the line too long. I've still got work for her to do."

"Yes sir." The line went momentarily dead then the love of my life was back.

"When are you coming home?" she asked before anything else.

"Looks like I'll be back by Monday; Sunday at the earliest," I said.

"Really?"

"Then pack your bags because we're off for a week."

"Really? Where to?"

"You pick a place and surprise me when I get back."

"Done."

I heard a click in my ear. Warton was signalling he needed her back.

"Time to go. I love you."

"Ditto." Then the line went dead.

Time to bring Peter Wilcox in.

I headed for my car. The traffic was moderately busy, so the ride back up to Stadacona took a few minutes longer which was okay. It gave me time to put together a plan of action.

First, I would detain him and take him into custody. One of the good things about the Secrets Act, it gave me limited powers where matters of national security were concerned; one of those powers was to take into custody anyone suspected of contravening the act. It also allowed me to hold them incommunicado indefinitely if necessary. A useful tool to squeeze information out of suspects.

Once I cleared the gate at Stadacona, I drove directly to the research building where Wilcox worked. I parked in front, got out and went inside where I was confronted by another armed sailor. I then made my way up the stairs to Wilcox's lab room. I spotted him standing with two other civilians bent over a large worktable with a set of drawings on it.

He did not see me approaching.

"Peter Wilcox," I said, showing him my identification and badge. "Step back from the table."

"Wh...what?" he said, turning to look at me with a startled look on his face.

"I am detaining you under the National Secrets Act. Come with me." I reached out and took hold of his arm.

"But...but, why? What have I done? You can't just..."

"I have the authority, which you would know if you read the conditions of your employment and the Act that you signed. Now, come along, there's a good chap," I said without stopping or looking at him as I forced him into motion.

"I demand to know why you are doing this?" he protested in a shaky voice.

He was obviously scared. Good.

I did not say anything, continuing to lead him out the door and down to the stairs. He kept demanding to know what was going on all the way to the car. I opened the rear door and signalled him to get in. He hesitated.

"We can do this the easy way or the hard way; your choice." I held out a set of steel handcuffs.

He stared at them for a moment then got into the car.

"Where are you taking me?" he asked.

Again, I did not answer him. I knew by keeping quiet it would rattle him, making him more 'pliable' once I got him into the interrogation room. During the drive back to

RCMP headquarters, I took several looks in the rear-view mirror. He definitely looked worried; scared.

When we arrived, I parked and got Wilcox out of the car. Holding his arm again, I led him into the building then upstairs to the interrogation room. As we passed by Carol's desk, I stopped and said, "Could you contact Lieutenant Commander Swanson and ask him to come down. Tell him that I have taken Peter Wilcox into custody and would appreciate his presence during the interrogation."

"Certainly, Inspector; right away," she said with a serious tone of voice as she reached for her phone.

"And have a constable come up to watch over him. He'll be the interrogation room. Thank you."

Five minutes later, I had Wilcox sitting in a windowless room with a constable standing by the door. I went to McKinnon's office. Carol informed me that Swanson was on his way.

"Show him in when he arrives and thanks again," I said. "You played that quite well back there."

"I think it sunk in with him," she said with a smile. "Nothing like official formality to unsettle someone, wouldn't you agree?"

"Absolutely."

"Coffee?"

"Let's wait until Swanson gets here; no sense in making two trips."

"Okay."

I went inside Bryon's office and took a chair.

"So, you picked him up?" he asked.

"He's down in the interrogation room. I had Carol call and invite Jules to come down and sit in, hope you don't mind?"

"Not at all. The more the better. If nothing else, it'll put the frighteners on him."

"That's what I'm counting on."

"Just how do you plan to go at him? Just so's I'll know what's what?"

"I think I'll begin with a little bluff, you know, give him a just a hint that we know something, like the missing documents from the records room with his name as the last entry in the logbook then proceed from there."

"What about using that lawyer's name, Simpson?"

"She's part of the plan, yeah," I said.

"This could be a very interesting day."

I sat back and smiled.

Jules Swanson arrived fifteen minutes later. Carol led him into the office. He took a seat as he shook hands with us.

"Coffees?" Carol asked before leaving.

"Excellent idea, thanks Carol," Bryon said.

"So, you have taken Mr. Wilcox into custody?" Swanson asked, looking from Bryon to me.

"I did, yes," I said.

"On what basis?"

"Everything I have so far is purely circumstantial, understand, but I'm satisfied that it's enough to act on."

"I see. Where is he now?"

"Down the hall in the interrogation room. I thought I'd let him stew for a while before I question him. He doesn't strike me as a hard case and perhaps this'll shake him up enough to get something out of him."

"And you wanted me here because...?

"If he does crack then whatever he tells us is going to directly fall under your jurisdiction as head of security. When you're done with him you can turn him back over to Bryon for any official criminal action."

Just then the door opened, and Carol came in carrying a tray with three mugs on it along with cream and sugar.

"Ah," Bryon said. "Just leave the tray, Carol, thanks."

She set it on the desk then turned and left. We each took a mug.

"Since this is your show, how do you want to handle it?" Jules asked.

"I was thinking 'good cop, bad cop'," I said, taking a sip of the coffee. "Hmm. Good coffee."

Jules gave me a questioning look.

"It's a police tactic the Yanks use," Bryon put in. "One of us leans on him with threats and other means of intimidation while another steps in offering a softer approach. From what I've heard, it's an effective tactic, especially on suspects who display nervousness or are scared."

"I see," Jules said. "And which of us is to play what role?"

"I think if the three of us confront him it'll have a great impact. I suggest that I play the bad cop and Bryon the good cop. I think we'll get quicker results if we tell him he's facing jail time either from us on criminal charges or from you from the security side. I'll hit him first with the charges of theft of government property and imply additional charges under the Security Act, namely, treason."

"Remind me not run afoul of you," Jules said. "You think it will work?"

"Pretty sure, if I've read him right," I said.

"Right. If we're agreed on our approach, what say we get the show on the road," Bryon said.

We got up and headed for the interrogation room. I picked up a large file from Bryon's desk as I stood up. He gave me a funny look.

"A prop," I said. "It'll make think we have compiled a dossier on him, and he won't know what it might contain

"Clever and a bit mean," he said. "I like it."

The constable standing over Wilcox eyed us when we entered and nodded.

"That'll be all, constable," I said, looking at him. "Why don't you go get a coffee. We'll take it from here.

Bryon and Swanson were already pulling chairs up to the table. I joined then, dropping the file on the tabletop with a bang. Wilcox flinched and looked very nervous and worried.

"You're in trouble, I said, lifting the cover of the file.

"What do mean? I haven't done anything wrong," he said in a slightly shaky voice, looking at the file.

"Not exactly true, is it? Does the records room ring a bell?"

"Records room?"

"According to the visitor's log, you were the only person to sign in on the day certain documents went missing. Care to explain that?"

"I don't know what you're talking about," he said, showing a little defiance. "I didn't take any documents."

"Then how do you explain the fact that you are the one that was there that day."

"I'm in there quite a lot, that doesn't mean I took any documents. Maybe they just got misfiled or lost."

"You believe that, do you?" I said leaning in. "Look. You got a chance here to help yourself. Start telling us what you know; who else is involved and the name of your Soviet contact and maybe, just maybe, we can do something; otherwise..." I left the rest of that statement hanging between us.

I saw he was starting to look even more nervous.

"Start with Caroline Simpson. Is she one of your connections to the Soviets?"

"You know about...? he started to say then clammed up.

"That's right, we know about her and your connection to her as far back as your college days."

"Mother of God," he muttered.

"Look, son," Bryon stepped in, speaking in a less confrontational tone of voice. "We understand you were just doing something you believed wasn't that serious and nobody would get hurt, but stealing secrets of any kind and passing them on to a foreign government has very serious penalties. What we're really interested in is who is working with you and the agents you report to. So, take a minute and think about it."

Wilcox looked like a trapped animal; his eyes darting rapidly from me to Bryon then to Swanson who was sitting quietly at the end of the table.

"Alright. What do want to know?"

"Tell us about Simpson," I said, slipping back into the conversation. "And about the couple staying at the Waverley Inn."

"She's not involved, as far as I know,' he said.

"Just a minute," Bryon cut in.

He stood up and went to the door, opened and leaned out and called for Carol.

"Carol. Can you come down here and bring your note pad."

He came back to the table and sat down.

"May as well get this down on paper.," he said, looking at me.

I nodded.

A few moments later, Carol came in and took a seat off to the side: pen and pad in hand.

"Right," I said, looking back at Wilcox. "Go on. You said she wasn't involved. You mean not involved in the passing of secret documents?"

"That's right," Wilcox said. "In fact, I didn't even know she was still active in the party. Not until she called me to help her find a safe place for a Russian."

"What Russian?" I asked.

"I don't know who he is. I never spoke to or met him before."

"And did you?"

"Did I what?"

"Find him a safe place?"

"Sort of, I mean, I assume it's a safe place. I don't usually go to such places myself. I only knew about the place from what I have heard."

"Give us a detailed description of this man and full details on where you took him," I said.

When he finished, I glanced at Carol, "Get that?"

She nodded. At the same time, Bryon stood up and left the room. I reckoned he was headed for his phone to call Pete Duncan.

"Why would this Russian go to her and need to find a safe place?" I asked.

"I don't know," he said. "I didn't ask; I didn't really want to know, but I think he must've known about her."

"What makes you think that?"

"In nineteen-fifty-two, I attended a seminar put on by Dalhousie concerning the place of Communism in world. That's when I saw Caroline. It was the first time since we graduated. Anyway, we spent the weekend together, you know, listening to the speakers then later, you know... It was on the last day when she told me about meeting a delegate from the Soviet embassy in Ottawa."

"What then?"

"That's it. She invited me to meet him, but I passed."

"So, no one contacted you the whole time you were there?"

"Well, uh, I did meet this one man. He wasn't one of the speakers, but said he was with the delegation as part of their security. Anyway, we got along really well and before he left he asked if I would be interested in helping the cause, I didn't think much about it, so I said sure."

"What was his name?" I asked.

"Josef Sokolov."

"Okay," I said. "Now, tell me about these people at the Waverley?"

I wrote down everything he said, including how many documents he passed on and over what time frame. Fortunately, it was not that many, but it was enough, and all of it had to do with the ASW research being carried out.

When he finished, I glanced quickly at Swanson who had been sitting quietly listening and gave him a slight nod.

"Tell us about Captain Jerome Carew's involvement?" he asked.

"I don't know him, oh, I've heard about him, but never actually met him," Wilcox said. "He worked in a different area from me."

"So, as far as you know the captain is not part of your little group?"

Wilcox shook his head.

"I have another question for you," I said cutting back in. "Why did Caroline Simpson call you to help find a place for this Russian, and how did the Russian know to contact her?"

"She called me because she knew I was still sympathetic to the Communist cause. As for why the Russian went to her, I don't know. Like I said, she said she had a contact in Ottawa. That's it."

At this point Bryon returned and took his seat again. He gave me a quick nod, indicating that he spoke with Duncan.

I closed over my notebook and started to stand.

"What's going to happen to me?" Wilcox asked, sounding scared.

"You'll be turned over to the security services," I said. "It'll be up to them what to do with you. If it were up to me, I'd throw the book at you and send you away for the rest of your life. There's nothing worse than a traitor."

I said this deliberately to keep the fear in him. I turned to Swanson who was standing now. "He's all yours. I'll be going after the woman next, so expect one more, at least."

"Right," Swanson said, then looking to McKinnon, asked, "Can you hold him here until I can make arrangements to transfer him to the brig up on the base?"

"Not a problem," Bryon said, signalling to Carol. She came over. "Get a constable back up here to guard him. Oh, and have that transcript typed up, and make copies."

"Yes sir, "she said, then turned and left.

The three of us left the room a moment later with Bryon locking the door and followed Carol back to Bryon's office.

"That went well," I said as we all sat down.

"Bloody good show," Swanson said, smiling. "Mind if I use the phone?"

"Go ahead," Byron said, gesturing to the phone.

"I'll have a shore patrol detachment come down and collect him."

"Now what?" Byron asked, sitting down.

"Up for another interrogation?" I said with a smile.

"Absolutely."

"Good I'll be back in an hour. If it's okay with you, I'll take one of your constables with me."

"Go ahead."

Swanson hung up the phone and said the shore patrol would be here presently.

"Did I just hear that you are going after the Simpson woman?" he asked, looking at me.

"Uh-huh," I said.

"In that case, if you chaps don't mind, I think I'll stay around."

"Happy to have you," Bryon said, glancing at me. I nodded.

"Right. I'm off," I said and headed for the door.

I returned an hour and half later with a very pissed off Caroline Simpson in cuffs being led down the hall to the interrogation room. I noticed there wasn't a constable standing guard, so, after removing the cuffs and pacing her in the room, I instructed the constable I had taken with me to watch her. I left her sitting there, glaring at me, as I headed for Bryon's office.

Chapter Eighteen

Jesse Thompson

Bryon and Jules Swanson were sitting at his desk when I came in; each with a mug of coffee.

"I'm assuming Wilcox is on his way to the brig?" I said, moving to a n empty chair and sitting down.

"Fifteen minutes ago," Bryon said. "How'd you make out?"

"She's down in the room under guard," I said. "Don't expect too much cooperation out of this one, though. She's definitely going to be a tougher nut to crack. Remember, she's a lawyer and will be using that against anything we try."

"If I judge your face rightly, I'm guessing you got a plan in mind?"

"Could say that, yeah. You remember me saying that I operate under a different area of authority? Well, as such, I can arrest and detain indefinitely, anyone suspected of being engaged in any activities that contravene our national security. In fact, Jules here has similar powers, right?" I said, looking at him.

"To the large degree, yes, but I do not think it reaches quite as far as those granted to you."

"I not so sure," I said. "Granted, I may be pushing the envelope a little..."

He looked at me with a raised eyebrow.

"So, you plan to push it with her?" Bryon asked.

I smiled.

"Well let's have at it then and see how tough she really is?"

We stood and headed to the interrogation room.

"I demand that you release me immediately," she said, angrily. "You had no right or authority to arrest me, or to keep me here."

"In fact," I said as we took our seats at the table," "you're wrong. I have the authority under the National Secrets Act to arrest and detain without warrant, anyone suspected of being engaged in criminal or treasonous acts against the interests of the country."

I studied her face as I made this little speech, watching for any crack in her demeanour. Then I saw it...a slight flicker, a tiny movement in her eyes; the crack.

"What the hell are you talking about? What do mean treason?" she demanded, raising her voice.

"Tell us about this Russian that called on you to help him find a safe place to stay?" I asked, ignoring her outburst.

"I don't know anything about any Russian," she said with just a hint of a catch in her voice.

"We know that you were contacted by this man, and we know that you also enlisted the aid of Peter Wilcox in finding this man a safe hiding place. We know where he was taken and local the police authority is preparing to pick him up."

"You can't do that," she said, "he's a client and I demand that..."

"You are in no position to make any demands," I said cutting her off. "This man is suspected in the brutal murder of an elderly woman yesterday. In addition, he is also suspected of being a Soviet agent here on a specific mission. Now, he may have come to you as a lawyer for help on the first charge, but not on the second which makes you complicit in espionage."

That shut her up. She sat there looking at each of us in turn; you could almost hear the wheels turning in her mind as she assessed her situation. I did not want to give her time to recoup.

"This man here is Lieutenant Commander Jules Swanson with Naval Intelligence. In a few moments you will be surrendered to his custody and charged under the National Secrets Act for acts of espionage. But first, you will tell us everything about your connections with the Soviets network and your contacts in Ottawa."

"I have nothing more to say, except I want a lawyer."

She sat back in the chair and folded her arms defiantly across her chest and glared at me.

"Suit yourself," I said, standing up. "Just remember the Rosenbergs." That seemed to shake her up a bit.

They were an American couple who were exposed as Soviet agents, charged and then convicted of espionage. There were found guilty and executed in the electric chair on June 19th, 1953, at Sing Sing Federal Penitentiary. That, I noticed, shook her up just a little. We left the room to allow her to stew for a bit.

"Jesus, you really laid it on in there," Bryon said when resumed our seats from before outside the interrogation room.

"She needed to understand that she doesn't carry any weight here," I said with a shrug. "Besides, she rubs me the wrong way."

"I wasn't criticizing; just not used to handling a woman that way. I get why you did it. So, you really going to turn her over to Jules here?"

"Don't see why not. It is his bailiwick, after all. I made it clear from the start my only interest was to identify and shut down any possible security breaches within the research departments. I think I have done that, so my work here is just about over. The rest falls to you and Jules. All's that's left is

237

to bring in the two agents staying at the Waverley Inn."

"Well, from where I sit, you have done a great piece of police work, and I am most grateful," Jules said. And now gentlemen, if you will allow me, I think I'll collect my latest prize and leave you to your deliberations with my hearty thanks."

He stood up and extended his hand to me which I accepted, then over to Bryon.

"I'll call you first of the week," he said, shaking his hand. "Let's get together and you can fill me in on how you made out."

"That would be fine," Jules said, letting go of his hand. "Let's say lunch in the Officer's Mess. My treat, of course. You too, if you are still here," he said this last bit to me.

"Thanks," I said, "but I plan to be either back in Ottawa or somewhere between here and there by then."

"Then safe journey," he said, putting on his white brimmed cap and black greatcoat.

Bryon and I watched him leave.

"There's goes a decent chap," I said when the door closed.

"Yep...for a Brit," Bryon said. "Okay, now what?"

"When was the last time you made an arrest?"

"Now?" he said, smiling.

"Good a' time as any," I said, standing up. "With what Wilcox gave us I think I got enough to bring them in."

"Let's go, then."

Just at that moment Carol knocked on the door and stepped inside.

"Yes?" Bryon said, standing behind his desk.

"You're not going to believe this," she said, her eyes wide, "there are two people outside, a man and a woman, claiming to be Soviets wanting asylum."

"Jesus," Bryon said.

"What do I do? I have never dealt with a situation like this before." Carol asked.

"Whaddya think?" he asked, looking me.

"Take them to the interrogation room," I instructed her. "Make sure they're comfortable and offer them something to drink. I'll be along in a few minutes."

"Okay," she said and turned away, closing the door behind her.

"I'll take it from here, if that's okay with you?" I said to Bryon.

"Be my guest," he said, sitting back down. "Want me to get Jules back?"

"Not yet. This might be out of his area. I don't think he's set up to deal with possible defectors. Once I find out what exactly is going on, I'll call Ottawa. You want to sit in?"

"Yeah, if you don't mind. Be interesting to see how this goes."

We left his office and went to the room and our 'guests'.

Josef Sokolov and Ivanka Chenko sat close to each other at the wooded table. They seemed composed and relaxed, looking directly at us as we came in and took our seats opposite them.

"I'm Inspector Jesse Thompson," I opened, "and this is Inspector Bryon McKinnon."

"Josef Sokolov and this is my wife, Ivanka Chenko," the man said. "We are Soviets who wish to defect to the west."

"I see," I said. "First, I have to ask you some questions. Are you willing to provide the answers?"

"Da, er, yes. We will cooperate as far as we can go."

"What do mean by that?"

"We are, as I am sure you already now, agents with the GRU. I, we, are willing and ready to answer any questions related to our mission and to such missions we know about, but not our state secrets. We are defectors, not traitors."

"Well, let's start there for now," I said. "I am an investigator with our internal intelligence division. You will have to be turned over to another department for de-briefing, understand?"

"Yes."

"Right. First order of business. What was your mission here in Halifax?"

"To obtain as much information of your navy's research and development on anti-submarine warfare systems."

"And just how were going to obtain that information?"

"Through contacts."

"These contacts, are they working inside the establishments and are they Soviet agents?"

"Yes, they are employed by your government and navy; no, they are not agents."

"How were they contacted?"

"Most were recruited years ago, many from the various universities, who have sympathies for the communist cause."

"I see. Will you tell us the names of all these contacts?"

"Yes."

"Next," I said. "Why did you decide to defect?"

"That is a difficult question," he said.

"We are loyal Russians," Ivanka said, speaking for the first time. "You must understand, for some of us, to be a Soviet is a political choice, but being a Russian is a birthright."

"I understand," I said.

"Good. It is important that you do. We have seen how the politics have changed since the war. Since Stalin's reign has ended. Now it has become corrupt and..."

I saw Sokolov place a hand on her knee, signalling her to stop.

"Let's us just say that we have become disaffected and no longer believe in the system," he said, looking at me.

"Fair enough," I said. "Your personal reasons are yours; my only interest at the moment, is the names of your contacts within our services."

He nodded.

"Are you the only agents here at the moment?"

"*Nyet*, there is another. His name is Pavlo Palyvoda; an assassin."

"Why is he here?"

"Most likely to kill us," Sokolov said bluntly without any emotion.

"Why would the GRU want to murder you?"

"We do not believe it is on GRU orders," Ivanka said.

"I don't understand?"

"We believe the order came from Sergi Agapov; a political officer at the embassy. A man with very dangerous ambitions," Sokolov said.

"I think I begin to see what you mean by being disaffected," I said.

"Do you now a woman; a lawyer, named Caroline Simpson?"

"We are aware of the name," Sokolov said. "I think she was recruited by Agapov years ago; possibly there was an affair."

I turned to Bryon, who was sitting there taking all this in. "Can you call Carol to come in and take their deposition and the names of the contacts?"

He nodded and stood up, went to the door and left. Shortly thereafter, he returned with Carol close on his heels. She had a tray with two fresh mugs of coffee and a tape recorder on it. I got up and looked down at the pair.

"Please give everything you have to this lady. She will record it on that machine. I will return once you're done, agreed?"

"We understand," Sokolov said as Carol set the mugs in front of them. "A question, If I may ask?"

"Yes?'

"When we are done what will become of us? We cannot go back to the Inn, I think."

"You will be put under our protection supervised by Inspector McKinnon here," I said.

"Then you will be taken from here to a safe location under military authority until we receive instructions from Ottawa. You will be safe and comfortable," Bryon said, taking over. "Come see me when you've finished up here," he said this to Carol. Then he and I headed back to his office.

"Now what the hell do make of that?" he asked as we sat down.

"Unexpected," I said, but a stroke of dumb luck I'd hafta say."

"No shit. I take it this means your mission is over?"

"More or less, yeah. I'll stick around for another day in case there are any loose ends needing to be dealt with like..."

"This Palyvoda business?" Bryon said, finishing my thought.

"Uh-huh. By the way, you hear anything more from Pete?"

"I touched base with him, and he says he's waiting on the Crown Attorney's office to come up with a warrant."

"Hmm. Sometimes I forget what a pain in the ass 'red-tape' is and the crap you gotta go through."

"All part of police work," he said with a sigh. "Better that than lose the guy on a technicality."

"Good point."

Chapter Nineteen

Pavlo Palyvoda

Pavlo Palyvoda stood in a doorway across the street from the entrance to the Waverley Inn patiently waiting. He had been given the order to eliminate Sokolov and Chenko.

He had spent over an hour watching the Inn for the Sokolov's to make an appearance without much success. Finally, he decided to go inside and ask if they were actually in. The desk clerk said they left a few hours ago and, no, he did not where they went.

He left cursing his luck. Once back on the street, he stood considering his next move. There was no point in him looking for them since he had no idea where to even begin looking, so he headed back to his rooms. He would check back again later. At the worst, he would have to wait until tomorrow.

After a quick meal in the hotel diner, He decided to go out for a walk to clear his mind. Later, he found himself sitting at a small round table in a dimly lit corner of a local tavern with a half empty glass of tepid draught beer in front of him. He liked the taste; reminding him of beer he used to drink when he was in Britain just after the war.

He cast his eye around the room, taking in the trade. At this time of the evening, most of the drinkers were working men; dock workers or railroad men, there were a few he thought were fishermen and several street toughs. He noticed the marked absence of women, not surprising since learning that they were not permitted in taverns. Stupid idea, he thought, picking up his glass.

He signalled a passing waiter walking through the tables with a tray of glasses to bring another beer. When he set a glass down, he passed him a ten-dollar banknote.

"Sorry mate," the waiter said. "Ain't cha got anythin' smaller? It's only a quarter a glass."

Palyvoda pulled the note back and fished out a couple of coins from his pocket, dropping them on the waiter's tray.

"Thanks. Jus' a' head's up pal; I wouldn't go flashin' that kind of money 'round in here, if ya git me." Then he moved off to another table.

Palyvoda picked up the fresh glass and as he took a drink eyed the nearby tables to see if anyone was paying him any attention. Then he spotted them: three men he saw earlier sitting a few tables away. They were bent over their drinks in a huddle, talking.

He instinctively knew what they were scheming. He quietly chuckled to himself as he set the glass back down on the table.

In the meantime, he went over the conversation he had with Agapov earlier that day.

"I believe something is going on," Agapov said when he finished his report. "I think they may be up to something."

"Your orders, Comrade?"

There was a brief moment of silence, then, "Eliminate them."

"As you command, it will be done," he said, smiling.

"Return to Ottawa immediately it is done and report directly to me."

"Comrade."

Then the line went dead.

He picked up the glass and finished the beer. He stood up and went into the toilet. Once inside, he adjusted his overcoat so he could move more freely and reach his weapon. When he came out he noticed they were gone. No surprise, he thought. The way he worked it out was they had to be waiting somewhere outside to see where he was going to go before making their move.

He headed for the door. Standing on the sidewalk outside the tavern door, he turned and started to walk down the street. It was dark now and the street was dimly lit by low watt lamps, so there were plenty of shadows as well as deep alleys between the buildings.

He was about thirty feet down the sidewalk when he heard them. This was going to be too easy, he thought, as he reached the corner and turned right. He spotted an alley ten feet away and quickly moved to it, stepping just inside into the shadow.

The three men moved past the entrance of the alley then stopped.

"Where da fuck he git to?" one asked.

"Right here, comrades," Palyvoda said as he stepped out of the shadows with a stiletto in his hand that was held beside his leg. "You want something, da?"

The three turned in unison with startled looks on their faces. No one noticed the knife.

"Whaddya know, fellas, a Gawd damn Commie," one of them said as they quickly recovered and slowly moved apart. He was the biggest of the three. Heavily built but showing signs of too much beer and bad food. The other two looked typical street thugs. One of them held a leather sap in his hand.

"Jus' hand over yer wallet," one said, holding out his hand. "Or else it'll go hard for ya."

"*Nyet*," Palyvoda said calmly. "I do not think so."

They started to spread apart then the big man stepped towards him with a hand reaching for him.

Palyvoda easily side-stepped to his left and at the same time lashed out with a foot, connecting viciously with the man's forward knee, pushing it back at an unnatural angle.

"A-a-a-a-a-a-a-a-a," the man screamed as he crumpled to the ground.

The move was so fast that others hesitated, giving him the time to swing the knife up and slash across the cheek of the one with the sap. He then set himself to face the last one.

"Jesus Christ," he swore, taking few steps then turned and ran down the street.

Palyvoda stood a moment, looking at his handiwork then turned and walk backed the way he came. "*Lyubiteli.*" He spat as he stepped over the fallen man.

Back at the Inn, he was told the Sokolovs still had not returned. He did not see the two men in overcoats come into the lobby until one of them said, "Pavlo Palyvoda. Place your hands on the counter and spread your legs. You're under arrest."

He slowly looked over his right shoulder and saw one of the men was holding a gun levelled at him. The other man stepped carefully up to him with a pair of handcuffs in his hand.

"Hands behind your back," the second man said, reaching for his left arm.

Palyvoda offered no resistance. He just stared at the desk clerk who had moved away from the desk, pressing himself against the wall with a half dozen cubby holes at his back.

"My name is Detective Duncan and I'm arresting for the murder of Mrs. Shirley Jacobs two days ago. Anything you say will be taken down and may be used against you at trial. Do you understand?"

Palyvoda said nothing, did nothing.

* * *

Pete Duncan

"Pat him down, then put him in the car," Pete said to the other detective. "I'll be out in a few minutes."

The detective did as he was told and patted him down, retrieving a gun and the secreted stiletto from inside the arm of the jacket.

"Right," the detective said to him, grabbing his arm, leading him out of the building.

"Thanks Frankie, ya did good," he said to the night clerk. "What about them other two, they in?"

"No," the clerk said, looking shaken. "They left 'bout mid-afternoon and ain't come back."

"Okay, an' thanks again. I owe ya a big one."

"Anytime, Pete. Anytime. Jesus he's was a scary sonnofabitch."

Back at the station, Palyvoda was relieved of his belt and shoes then put into a holding cell. Pete went back to his desk after officially booking Palyvoda in. He picked up the phone and dialed Bryon McKinnon's number. No answer. He looked up at the wall clock – ten-fifteen. He redialed the number for the dispatcher and got through. He identified himself and asked him to contact McKinnon at home and ask him to call the station as soon as possible then hung up.

Ten minutes later his phone rang.

"What's up?" McKinnon asked.

"I got Palyvoda in custody," Pete said without any preamble.

"Really? When did you take him?"

"An hour ago. He's been booked for murder, jus' wanted to let you know so you can pass it along to Jesse."

"Will do, and great job by the way."

"Thanks. Couldn'a done it without your help."

"That's what cops to do; help each other, after all, getting the bad guys is what we do."

"Damn straight. Well, I'll let ya go an' call ya tomorrow."

"Okay, tomorrow." Then the line went dead.

Pete felt tired but pleased at the same time. He always felt good when he caught the really bad ones without any one of his men, or an innocent citizen, getting hurt. He grabbed his coat and hat then headed for the parking lot and home where he would embrace the only truly important thing in his life: his wife.

***

Jesse Thompson

The next morning, after breakfast, I was back in my room making final preparations for my departure back to Ottawa when the phone rang.

"Mornin' sir," the young sounding man said. "A call came in from an Inspector McKinnon while you were in the dining room, asking you to call him."

"Thanks," I said. "Get me an outside line, please."

"Yes sir, right away." The line went dead for a moment then I heard a dial tone and dialed Bryon's number. He picked up on the third ring.

"Inspector McKinnon," he said.

"Mornin', it's me, Jesse," I said. "You called?"

"Yeah. Got some good news thought you'd like to hear."

"Must be good if you're in the office on a Saturday."

"I got a call from Pete Duncan late last night. He's made an arrest in that murder case. Guess who?"

"Palyvoda," I said.

"You got it."

"Anyone get hurt?"

"Nope. According to him, the Russian just gave up. He's in the lock-up at the station. Pete's probably going to keep him on ice until Monday when he can start proceedings with the Crown. He's been formally charged and booked for the murder."

"That's great news," I said. "Pass along my congrats when you talk to him again."

"So, that mean you have no more interest in Palyvoda?" Bryon asked.

"That's right, actually, I never did have any interest beyond helping to catch him. As far as I am concerned this is a local matter to be dealt with by Duncan and you, if it comes to that. My mission ended when the Sokolovs surrendered themselves to you for asylum and gave up the people on the Soviet's payroll. In fact, this business ended better than I could've hoped for. Jules has the means now to clean house of some bad actors and Ottawa has a couple of key players willing to shake up the Soviet networks. All-in-all a good day's work, you'd agree?"

"Absolutely," Bryon said. "So, you're away then? When?"

"I'm going to see if I can hitch a ride on a military transport first, then, failing that, book a commercial flight for later today."

"So, that means you got time for a last lunch; on me, as a farewell?"

"Definitely," I said, smiling.

"Good. Call me when you've made your arrangements then I come get you. Afterwards, I'll run you to either Shearwater or the airport."

"Appreciate it, and the friendship. I'll get back to you."

He said he would be staying at the office for the while, but gave me his home number just in case he left.

Epilogue

Jesse Thompson

Two days after I returned to Ottawa, I learned that Josef Sokolov and Ivanka Chenko were transferred from Halifax to a secret location in Ontario where they were being de-briefed by military intelligence officers and new identities and lives were being prepared for them.

Bryon called and told me that, despite very angry protests by the Soviets demanding that Palyvoda be released to them, the Crown was able to keep their hold on him and preparations were underway to bring him to trial for first degree murder. If convicted, Palyvoda was looking at a life sentence in our maximum-security penitentiary, which would seem like a country club compared to what I have heard about Russian gulags.

I later learned that he turned and gave our intelligence service information in exchange for a reduced sentence. The wheels of political intrigue roll on. However, while in prison awaiting a transfer, Palyvoda was found dead in his cell. He had been killed by a stab in the heart. The case remains unsolved.

He also reported that Peter Wilcox has been charged under the National Secrets Act and was currently awaiting trial. Caroline Simpson had also been charged as an accessory in the murder of Shirley Jacobs and the Crown had petitioned the Nova Scotia Barrister's Association to disbar her and revoke her licence. Jules Swanson told me that Captain Jerome Carew was given the opportunity to quietly resign his position and commission in exchange for keeping his military pension and would be given a letter of recommendation. He accepted and moved away.

The good news is that by the time I received the okay for the long-promised week off, Marie Chassion and I were married and the vacation became a honeymoon.

The End

Appendix
Abbreviations
Canadian Agencies

DSTIDirectorate for Scientific and Technical Intelligence

DRBDefence Research Board

NRCNational Research Council

NRENaval Research Establishment

SOSUSSound Surveillance System Under Sea

Soviet Agencies

GRUSoviet Domestic and Foreign Intelligence Service

KGB Komitet Gosudarstvennoy Bezopasnosti (1954 – 91)

Note: The KGB is divided into 20 directorates, the most important

were those responsible for foreign intelligence, domestic counter-

intelligence, technical intelligence and safety of leaders and borders.

ASW Systems

VDSVariable Depth Sonar

TASSTowed Array Sonar System

CANTASSComputer signal processor

SOFARUnder sea sound fixing and ranging channel

LOFARLow frequency analysis and recording computer

Places of Note

HMCS Dockyard, Halifax, Nova Scotia location of east coast fleet

HMCS Stadacona, Halifax, Nova Scotia location of navy's land-based operations and command

HMCS Shelburne, Shelburne, Nova Scotia main link with US Navy's SOSUS ASW system

Halifax Shipyards, Halifax, Nova Scotia site for installing new ASW systems – private company

RCMP HQ Halifax, Nova Scotia 203 Hollis Street

H. Paul Doucette lives in Dartmouth, Nova Scotia. After a life-long career in transportation, first as a merchant seaman then as an industrial logistics specialist, he embarked on a journey of artist discovery. He has had moderate success as a fine art photographer and now as an author with over twenty novels to his credit.

He has combined his love of history and mysteries to create several well researched fictional series with settings ranging from Prohibition and World War Two to the counterculture years of the nineteen sixties and seventies.

At the present, he is developing another new series set in Canada during the Cold War.

BWL Publishing

bwlpublishing.ca

The following is a list of available titles from BWL Publishing Inc.: bookswelove@telus.net.

The John Robichaud Mysteries set in Halifax during WWII
Dead Man In The Harbour
Murder on The Docks
The Body In Room 103
The Evil Men Do
The Norwegian Woman
Robie's War
Robie's Last Case

The Matt Murphy Mysteries set in Toronto in the 1960/70s
Step Softly Ere You Go
Revenge
No Time For Hate

Canadian Historical Mysteries #1 (Nova Scotia) BWL Publishing Inc.
Rum, Bullets and Cod Fish: A Prohibition Story